The Criminal at Large

A novel

The Criminal at Large
A novel

Ramachandra Behera

Translated by
Jagannath Dash

BLACK EAGLE BOOKS
2021

 BLACK EAGLE BOOKS

USA address:
7464 Wisdom Lane
Dublin, OH 43016

India address:
E/312, Trident Galaxy, Kalinga Nagar,
Bhubaneswar-751003, Odisha, India

E-mail: info@blackeaglebooks.org
Website: www.blackeaglebooks.org

First International Edition Published by
BLACK EAGLE BOOKS, 2021

THE CRIMINAL AT LARGE
by **Ramachandra Behera**

Cover & Interior Design: Ezy's Publication

ISBN- 978-1-64560-184-5 (Paperback)
Library of Congress Control Number: 2021938760

Printed in United States of America

To

All the unfortunate mothers and sisters
who are between to be or not to be

Translator's Note

After reading Ramachandra Behera's *Nikhoj Aparadhi*, the most compelling contemporary Odia novel in a single sitting I made a phone call to him. I wanted just to congratulate him for having conceived such a brilliantly powerful plot which had been so well expressed through patterns of words like tapestries creating delicate and flawless verbal rhythms. I was enchanted and spell bound for a long time. Its hangover continued for days together in me; the question- 'was such a mother character ever possible', and 'could there ever be any greater woman issue than this' rang in my ear making me restless. By the by, I asked the writer how he conceived such a character named Chhaya. He said he had not created her; he had met her on the pages of the Newspaper. Such a mother was there in flesh and blood who had surrendered her criminal son to the Police. It happened in Balasore. To my surprise, he said that he had written the novel being possessed by that theme. I read it once again. Reading this novel was as good as seeing life in its different forms and dimensions that are so pitiable and handicapped and yet so glorious and powerful! I felt the necessity of sharing the pleasure with non-Odia readers by rendering it into English.

Rama Chandra Behera, a frontline literary celebrity has a strong claim to being one of the best fiction writers in Odisha. He has been showered with a number of accolades and encomiums including the prestigious Atibadi Jagannath Das award; but the works of such a great genius are not that known among the non-Odia readers outside Odisha. The other reason for translating 'Nikhoj Aparadhi' is its socio-ethical relevance to the present-day women themes that are of paramount concern all over our country.

Translating Rama Chandra Behera is not easy because the lyrical fictionist provides intensely pleasurable and painful private experiences while his stories discover man's emotional and intellectual entity and paint the human passion with strange colours on a wide canvas of reality. Further, his mellifluous language impregnated with both philosophical and romantic energy, and his extraordinary narrative style and technique pose the real challenge to the translator. I have tried to be true and honest to the spirit of the text.

I am immensely thankful to Rama Chandra Behera for having permitted me to translate his novel 'Nikhoj Aparadhi' into English. I am grateful to him in more ways than one. My sincere thanks are due to Manoranjan Mishra who went through the manuscript and helped me with his valued suggestions.

I express my heartfelt gratitude to Mr. Satya Pattanaik, Black Eagle Books, Dublin, USA for his generous gesture in accepting the manuscript for publication.

I will feel amply rewarded if the readers find it worth reading.

Jagannath Dash

The Criminal at Large

ONE

Vicky left home at 8 in the morning. He knew there would be a delay in his return. It would not be possible to reach home by lunchtime. So he asked his wife to have her lunch without waiting for him.

Within a month or so of her marriage, Vicky's wife had already become familiar with her husband's busy lifestyle. On some days Vicky would miss his lunch and on some other days, the dinner as well. The cell phone would bring the message about some incident or accident taking place somewhere. Attending to those would be urgent and important. He felt at that time that he wasted a lot of time in eating. While gulping down the dishes, he would ask his wife why she served so many items. Was it a trick to detain him at home for longer hours?

His cell phone would ring at odd hours during the post-lunch siesta on a programme-free day or at nine o'clock at night or during the early hours before daybreak. Incidents and accidents occur at no pre-fixed hours. They may visit any time. When normal life stumbles somewhere sometimes, that becomes news for others. To capture the events in his camera, Vicky would rush to the spot.

He has to travel a lot.

On that day, he had been out on his bike. A feud had cropped up between the supporters of two political parties.

Five to six houses had been burnt. Fifteen persons from both sides had been injured. A small boy was missing. Four cattle had been burnt alive. The irony was that the conflict hadn't taken place between two villages; it was the terrible outcome of the bitterness and animosity existing among the villagers.

Vicky would visit that village first to collect fresh news how things fared. Then, covering a distance of 15 km along a miserably rough road, he would ride on to another village. The eldest son of the family that he was going to visit was a schizophrenic. He went crazy suddenly when he was doing his matriculation. He chased and attacked all he came across. He set fire on two or three houses. His terror came to an end the day he rushed to finish his mother with a crowbar. He has been chained and confined in a dark room for the last seven or eight years. As he is caged, he doesn't look like a man. He looks strange and wild with animal-like behaviour. A rare story, certainly!

An acquaintance of Vicky had talked about this the previous day. He would try to make a small documentary on this. If it were not too late, he would go to another village. A student who had lost his legs and the right hand in an accident achieved astounding success in the plus two commerce examination. It was only on the previous day that the results had been published.

Vicky used to write poems while he was a student in the college. The inspiration for writing poems came from the romantic scenes of Hindi films- the distant green hills crowned with white patches of clouds, wide open space, rainbows arching on the river and waterfalls, the parks adorned with colourful flowers and the embrace, hugging and rolling of the hero and the heroine on the green lawns. Vicky watched Hindi movies very often those days.

Although he had no relation with any girl, he used to daydream a lot keeping the girl of his fascination at the centre of his imagination.

The poems he wrote during that period had in them the moonlit night, the fragrance of flowers, the quivering lips, and odour of the sweat. His hostel magazine had published two of those poems. He consoled himself after leaving the college thinking that he had no faculty for writing poetry although he had the poetic sensibility. He could understand ordinary poems and was charmed by the beauty in them but could never write like that to the charm and delight of others.

A lot of struggle yielded him the post of a journalist in a private TV channel. He had to slog for hours there. He had to run from place to place even at odd hours. A tedious job! But of late, he has started loving this profession. The aqueous quartz of silky stream, the enchanting, pleasant dreams, and the cherished embrace-none of them could come into his camera lens. Life is full of all these experiences although life is not that alone. It's larger than that. Vicky admits that he cannot capture the variety and vastness of life in his camera reels.

Particularly, he cannot capture lives of human beings amid myriad sorrows, despairs and uncountable human wants. At times there are injustice and wrongdoing, anger and resentment; there too are creativity and the struggle for existence. Life appears so pitiable and handicapped at times and yet so glorious and powerful at the other!

That day he returned from those three villages by four in the afternoon. He sent these stories to the Editor. They would be telecast if selected on the basis of the social and human interest in them.

He felt exhausted. He changed and washed up. He

would enjoy his lunch leisurely even though it was cold. He would congratulate himself on having spent a successful day. At least, he had captured the pictures of small and big incidents in his video camera.

Possibly, his cell phone kept itself waiting kindly till the time his lunch was over comfortably. He had thought of lying down for sometime. But it was not possible. The mobile phone rang while he was wiping his hand.

- "Chhaya madam had come to the Police Station," a voice emerged from the other end. The second sentence was, "She will go back to her village Chandanpur now."

Chhaya madam and Police Station! Vicky could not connect the two. Expressing ignorance,he said, "Hello, which Chhaya madam are you speaking about?"

: What? Don't you know the issue relating to Chhaya madam?

Vicky could not understand whether the voice at the opposite end pitied his ignorance or expressed surprise.

: Sorry, you-

Was the phone disconnected or the person at the other end did not like to say anything more?

Vicky was engrossed in thoughts. No, he could not remember any Chhaya madam. He hadn't been to Chandanpur for the last one year. But perhaps there was some spice in it for the TV news. He didn't know who Chhaya madam was. None the less; her association with the Police Station might have been possible due to some unusual or untoward incident. What that incident might be! It was difficult to guess.

News items are often exciting and surprising. Hadn't it been so, life wouldn't have been so mysterious. Stirring elements of distrust create some events.

Vicky felt restless. Chandanpur was 15 km away from

there. A small obscure village! Besides, a Middle School and some old Shiva temples were there.

It was already four o'clock by then. Absentminded Vicky came out of the house.

Almost an hour later he reached Chandanpur—a sleepy, quiet, inert village. The trees were motionless, speechless and depressed like the thatched houses. As it were, all the thatched roofs tried to cover up their wants and despondencies down-faced. The eroding verandas and torn thatched roofs expressed poverty and utter helplessness. The streams of rainwater had drawn some lines on the walls; a poor village like any other!

Vicky's bike had slowed down along the village path. It was narrow. At some points beside the village path cows were tied. Tied bullocks also stood there listlessly, least interested in munching hay. The creepers crawled up on to the thatched roofs. Here and there were boys and girls in pants and frocks. The housewives were standing at the doors. An elderly woman was massaging a new-born baby.

Four men in *lungi* and turbans were discussing something in a whisper. They looked sombre. It was evident from their faces that they found some particular issue unpalatable and wanted to protest.

: "I am Vicky." Slowing down the bike to a halt but not getting down, Vicky revealed his identity with all humility. He added, "I work in a TV channel. I would be happy, if you please tell me where I can get Chhaya madam. I heard that she belongs to this village."

Two of them avoided him and expressed their disgust for her. Another charged at him and said, "Let her live in peace. Do you get it, eh? Let her live with her lot. Why have you come to disturb her?"

Vicky sensed something perturbing to have taken

place. His curiosity and anxiety were at the peak. The vexation and non-cooperation of the people became unimportant and secondary.

However, another person intervened, "Wait; leave it. Why do you speak to the gentleman like that? Please don't take offense of him. We, the people of the entire village, are in great distress. A terrible gale! Do you understand? We are not able to decide by what name we shall address Chhaya madam- a goddess or a monster. She doesn't belong to this part of the village. Go straight along that road. Her house is on the turning to your right on this road. The building with walls without plaster belongs to her. We heard that she had been to the Police Station. We can't say whether she has returned yet or not."

By that time, Vicky already had had a brisk and agitated blood circulation. Perhaps, he was going to meet a rare lady. Goddess or monster- what did they mean by that? Without wasting any time he desired to meet Chhaya madam who had become the subject of such controversy. Perhaps, by the time he reached her, all the journalists of other channels must have captured the story. He apprehended. Vicky rebuked himself for such an inexcusable delay.

That was the house, he conjectured. The road had a right turn there. The house without plaster stood beside the road. It had a grilled corridor with an iron gate in the middle. The lock on the gate indicated that there was none inside. The doors and windows of all the three rooms were shut. The door panels had not been painted. A bench and two moulded chairs lay on the veranda. A hedge was there at the back of the house.

The mango, banana, coconut and drum-stick trees

had grown taller. The front yard also had a fence around it. It had some mango, jackfruit and coconut trees too.

Beyond all doubts that was Chhaya madam's house.

There were four or five bicycles parked beside the road. Some eight or ten persons including a few children were there. Vicky paid due respect to a person looking educated and aristocratic, donning Dhoti and *kameez* although he didn't know him. All were looking serious and troubled,but there was a tinge of empathy in their appearances.

: "I am Vicky." He felt the necessity of introducing himself. "I'm a TV journalist. Isn't madam at home?"-he added.

In fact, what he said was a question- where has madam gone and when she was expected to return? It warranted an answer. But it had no impact on the gentleman. He didn't show any interest in Vicky either. Everyone knew the matter about Chhaya. That was a sensitive issue. Everybody was concerned and worried about that. If Vicky did not know of it until then, he must be nothing sort of a pitiably backward fellow. The gentleman's look gave such a message.

Vicky with drew from the gentleman. There was no doubt that an abnormal tension and quietude had enveloped the entire village. It weighed heavily on the entire atmosphere of the worried and speechless village.

The gentleman's disinterest and unwillingness to divulge anything could not discourage a curious person like Vicky; instead, he grew more anxious.

: "Sir, please answer a question or two." A blend of politeness and firmness was reflected in his voice.

: "What sort of answer do you seek?" There was displeasure in the speaker's tone. It looked as if the entire incident was self- explanatory and self- evaluating. The event in itself was its explanation; it hardly left any scope for any doubt. That was what the gentleman's question implied.

Wiping his face with the hanky, he heaved a sigh and said hesitatingly, "Her son absconded after committing rape. On being informed by the Police, the mother helped the police to arrest her criminal son. You say that you are the reporter on some TV channel. Have you ever heard about such an incident?"

Vicky turned into a petrified idiot. His exposure to the unheard of incident made him feel as if his ability to comprehend human beings had received a serious jolt. It added a glorious page to his understanding of human nature.

The people of the village were unable to ascertain whether Chhaya was a goddess or monster; whether she was normal or abnormal. She herself identified the criminal. The evil deed of the criminal had wiped out filial connections. No, usually it's not the way it goes. The son-identity dominates and over-shadows the evil deeds and the terrible crimes. Despite being a woman from where did Chhaya muster so much of courage and strength to abdicate her son?

: Sir, if youplease don't mind, may I know who you are." Vicky sounded more courteous.

: "Who am I?" He felt belittled. Still, he said rather listlessly, "I am the Head Master of the Middle School of this village. Ms. Chhaya is my colleague. Nay, perhaps I should have said that I am her colleague. Any other measure cannot describe her. This school, this village, the entire area and all of us will be known only on account of her. I declare it proudly that I am the headmaster of the school where Ms. Chhaya teaches."

Could he express the intensity of his love and regards in any better way? Was there a language more powerful and expressive than that? Vicky did not know. At least he could never have said so generously like that.

: "Perhaps she has gone to the Police Station for quite some time," Vicky said.

: "It appears she has gone there since the day the concept of Police Station materialized."There was fatigue in his voice. There was endless empathy too. He reiterated, "She has gone there since then, perhaps to return only after identifying all the rapists of the entire world."

Vicky marked a slight difference in his tone- "I am here waiting for her. I couldn't know when she left for the Police Station. Of course, she will come. I will meet her, and that will be a mark of reverence; that will be my bouquet of love for her."

Vicky had never been so enraptured in his life before. He felt a deep sense of respect and love for the lady he hadn't seen. But it was not possible to collect more information. A bike stopped in front of the house. A lady got down. A young man parked his bike and stood beside her.

: "Now you can go," said the lady. Vicky was sure the lady was Chhaya madam. She said further, "You took a lot of pain for me. They must be waiting for you at home. My dear, please don't ride too fast. Go. Be happy, take care."

The young man said, "Please have my telephone number. Whenever you want anything, please order me, ma'am. I would feel fortunate if I could be of some use to you."

: "Oh, sure," promised Chhaya. Her voice seemed heavy'.

"Must be feeling thirsty, would you have some water?"

: "No", the young man said. He stooped, touched her feet and swayed his palms over his head to collect the harvested blessings. He saw the Head Master while coming to the bike. He saluted him and sped away.

Only at that moment, she became aware of the Head Master's presence. She said, "Sir, I'm terribly tired and not in a position to say anything. We would be talking later."

: "Sure." He said and added further, "You need rest. I didn't come here to disturb you."

She threw a cursory glance over the people there. With the key from her purse, she unlocked the door, went in and shut it from inside. Subsequently,all the inner doors opened one after another. She disappeared within.

Vicky stood there speechless. He kept on watching the lock that swung from side to side like an exhausted pendulum. The wooden grille was shut. The doors that opened for a while were shut too. Chhaya was all alone therewithin.

Alone! Returning from the Police Station after an aeon she was alone and that too, having accomplished something inconceivable and surprising. The naked hands bereft of the clanging bangles, the unadorned forehead having lost the vermillion mark or the *bindi,* and the white saree and blouse conveyed that she was a widow. Perhaps that five feet two inch slim and fair complexioned lady was the teacher of the Middle School. That was Chhaya madam! What more? A goddess or a monster?

The light of the day was fading fast. At that very time, Vicky stood alone in front of the closed house. Within the house, there was the companionless Chhaya. What was her identity- teacher, mother, goddess, monster or Chhaya? Vicky could not make any head or tail as he had not known much. He folded his hands and said – "You are a mystery. No common man can understand you. You are a closed room, an enigma. You need no reception. You are much higher than that. Of what use is the bouquet; you are the fragrance. You are the attraction. Here I pick up the soil you trod on and smear it on my forehead as the best sort of sandal."

After she had closed the door from within, strange feelings came to Chhaya. She was in the dark. It was so dark that in that familiar room she could not know the exact location of the bed, the cupboard, and other things. Did they exist? She could not ascertain.

In the midst of darkness, how easily the familiar turns unfamiliar and strange!

As the indicator showed, power supply had not been disrupted. It was surprising indeed. Chhaya switched on, the light burned brightly, and the fan rotated. Not only did the darkness disappear, but also the ringing of the eerie sound that had enveloped her receded.

But another strange and persisting feeling overtook her. She had no idea how long she sat on a vehicle that sped up so madly up to the point of making one out of breath. Her heart seemed to stop due to the tremendous momentum. All on a sudden, the movement of the vehicle stopped unexpectedly. She stood on the floor of her own house trying to hold herself. Was she whirling round right from the day she had the power of cognition till that time? It was as if she had stopped the game of spinnin ground all of a sudden. At present, the universe seemed to move around her.

So she sat on the bed and waited to see when the mad movement would stop. She got up again after a long time. Everything was hazy. She wiped her eyes. She realized that she was feeling very thirsty. She could not remember as to whether there was water in the fridge. There was water. She was relieved. She drank some water and washed her face with the rest. She wiped her face with one corner of her saree and thought of washing her hands and legs in the washroom and changing. Neither before the deities nor before the *Tulsi* was any incense stick burnt since the previous day. Police Station, the lock up, and the gratifying look of the police occupied the whole day. Nothing else was there.

The stream of consciousness was breaking down. Thoughts diffused. An unprecedented inaction possessed Chhaya. It was difficult for one sitting on the bed to think of the next step- whether to fall flat as a mark of surrender to the day-old languor or to get up to finish the evening chores despite the fatigue?

Does anything really come to a close till life breath goes on or till the blood circulates in the veins and arteries? She got up. The windows opened. Everything on earth looked hazy under the dusky twilight. The shrill whistle of the cricket proclaimed that nothing had been silent. Nothing became motionless, nothing ceased. If one observed the music and the tempo, there wouldn't be any doubt that the house, its environment, and the entire world existed and all were vibrant in a careless rhythm although the ways were not understood. Chhaya went to the cupboard to change.

There was a knock at the grille. Chhaya felt irritated. She came out of the room. As there was no light, she could not recognize who it was. She switched on. Her niece, Sony's face, beamed at the other side. She was in *salwar-kameez*, a grown up girl ready for marriage. She looked serious and tearful.

: "How now- my darling, my mom?" That was Chhaya's common address to her niece, Sony. It was only a simple, affectionate query. She said, "Why don't you come in? Come, dear."

Sony came into the Bedroom and said, "Aunty, mother wants you to have dinner with us. I'll come here to take you by 9 o'clock. She has further enquired whether you have eaten anything in the evening."

: "Your mother was saying she had lumber pain," Chhaya said. "Why is she worried about me in such a condition? I'll prepare something." She added.

: "No, not at all. You won't have to do anything like that," Sony protested. I'll be here right at nine."

She was about to leave but paused for a moment. Perhaps she felt like asking her something. But she didn't. Chhaya knew what she wanted to ask. Who wouldn't be curious to know about her Police Station- experience?

Only curiosity? No. It was more than that. Utter persiflage!

People mocked her—irrespective of whether she was absent or present. They tookher for an object of entertainment. Occasional obscene gimmicks were very bitter and heartless. There was a clear suggestion that they considered her a cheap stuff.

To be face to face with this was not a matter of joke. She couldn't ever understand why people gazed at her with disparaging looks. Was it ever possible to regard these as trifle junks? How could the views and attitudes of the mass, irrespective of time and place, be expected to be refined and ethical?

Oh, what agony one has to undergo for that! Tears roll down not from the eyes alone but ooze out of the entire body. The inner being bleeds!

She knew the reason why people like her had to pay a high price to thrive and safeguard their existence, although she found no justification in that. Of course, man's nature is like that. Sometimes it is godly and sometimes devilish. It is the rule of conscience, and sheer a mad passion at times. Both the self-alleviation and the mustering of courage as a preparation to counter the upcoming moment become incredibly excruciating.

So, it was not that unnatural on Sony's part to be curious about her experience at the Police Station. Sony was her close kindred. She was born after three or four years of her marriage.

She was the only child of her husband's elder brother. She was born after a lot of ritualistic practices. The labour pain was such that there was scarcely any hope of the survival of her *apaa*. There was no proper road or conveyance facility then. Very few automobiles pliedalong the way. However, to their good luck, a jeep could be arranged, with some difficulty though. To all the family members, it was nothing but a miracle. Not known how, perhaps as per the Almighty's desire, that jeep arrived in the village and transported *appa* to hospital.

This *appa*, her sister-in-law was Sony's mother. Abhaya, her husband's elder brother was Sony's father. Chhaya had lost all hopes and dreams of a marriage. She was prepared to spend her life in teaching-doing the blackboard and correction work. The school bell would be dividing her time from one period to another and from one academic year to another.

Thus she would pass her life.

She had her job. That was the support for her to hold on and to walk on. That would give her confidence. What else? There was her misfortune, her bad name. Would she end her life being afraid of that? Why was she preparing herself to destroy herself?

All these would make an epic. The marriage with Amiya in a temple only with the exchange of two ordinary garlands, indistinct chanting of mantras by the priest, blowing of conch shells, sacrificial fire and wedlock which followed by a *prasad* party. Sure, it was a surprising episode.

The most important event of life was all over within an hour.

Chhaya set out for her in-law's house as a pillion rider on Amiya's motorbike. Four or five accompanied them by scooters. She arrived at her husband's house which then had a thatched roof.

Amiya married Chhaya. The entire small village shook with protests and ridiculous comments. Amiya had married her keeping the probable ostracism in view. But, obliging and overwhelming him, his brother and sister-in-law extended their free hands of cooperation. Only within a very short time of ten minutes, all arrangements for a brief reception of the groom and bride were made. It was a warm and cordial welcome. Loving rebukes were showered on Amiya for having concealed such an important thing.

All these belonged to past.

Chhaya failed to realise when she had prepared tea or sipped it. She saw the cup after finishing it. Washing it, she kept it in the kitchen and wiped her hand.

It was half past eight. Without waiting for Sony, she locked up. The torch showed the road in front.

The tile-roofed house of Abhaya was there only within a distance of one hundred meters. Chhaya had never been eager to peep into the history of this family. But, at the time of her marriage, Abhaya and Amiya were living separately. She did not know any bitterness prevailing between the two brothers. Out and out, her *appa* was an emotional and affectionate person. She wondered why they separated.

Abhaya was sitting with two other persons on the cement veranda. Seeing her, he said, "Sony was to go there to call you. It's good, you have already reached. Go in."

Abhaya is a man of few words. From the beginning, he had never behaved as the elder brother of her husband (*dedhashura*) but as her own elder brother.

It was a three-roomed house with the kitchen at the left and a concrete courtyard. The altar of *Tulsi* was at the centre of the courtyard. The corridor connected to the kitchen by a wall to the right.

As usual, Chhaya went to the kitchen. Sony was busy doing something there. As a matter of habit, she said to Sony, "You go and enjoy watching TV with your mother. I'll do the rest of the things here."

: "I'd have gone to call you within five to ten minutes." Sony said, "Better you go and sit with mother. Everything is complete."

Appa, coming out of the TV room said, "You must be tired, as such, you needn't have to cook here. Come and sit with me."

: "You had lumber pain, have you come round? Chhaya sat on the bed.

: "Do you think it will be alright? She sounded pessimistic. She said further, "With medicines, there is a little relief. After two or three days it resurfaces."

: "*Appa,* I would like to massage your leg. That was a sort of appeal to get her permission. A little pressure on your back would give you some comfort. I came earlier to do this."

Appa looked at Chhaya. Chhaya was always like that, generously affectionate.

Only but a few can express the loving intimacy so beautifully; touch the heartstrings so well to create the vibrant music. Of course, Chhaya looked exhausted after such a terrible incident, but there was no sign of repentance in her for what she had done.

What is she -a goddess or monster? Such type of debate had been going on, unresolved. Was there any element of a monster in her?

How and where does it get expressed?

Appa had not got any trace of it. Perhaps, she had never been interested to find that out.

She replied to Chhaya's appeal. She moved her hand smoothly over her head and cheeks and on her body. Just on seeing Chhaya, she had started smiling, but this smile got itself converted into tears. Her face contracted. Her lips throbbed for words that did not get any vent to escape. Her aching waist could not check the violent trembling.

Cupping her palms *Appa* held Chhaya's face in them. With much difficulty, she uttered, "Chhaya, my dear, how come all misfortunes befall on you! What else is left for you to undergo? It's harrowing to think of what you have undergone."

Chhaya was prepared to see or listen to something like this. Her appa was like that. She often got impatient and burst into tears at some unexpected mishaps. Chhaya did not say anything. She kept on gazing at appa's crying face.

: "Please ask Chhaya if I would ask someone to sleep in her house." Abhaya asked standing on the veranda.

: "I'll manage myself." Said Chhaya who had been well- acquainted with the chronic loneliness. With a tinge of melancholy, she added, "What else is left there for the thieves to steal? In case of any difficulty, I'll inform you."

Two

Mohangarh was not such a sleepy and inert village when Chhaya was in the seventh class.It seemed to be getting up and to be frolickingand frisking about. It was just becoming conscious of itself and was basking at the prospect of getting transformed into a town. Every day new features were getting added in that direction. Dreams were getting accumulated in the wakeful village for developing a trade centre in that area.

The main road ran through the middle of the village and the routes to all the adjacent villages originated from this village. The people of these villages could go easily to Mohangarh for marketing and for catching buses to the District Headquarters. There was good communication from there to the state capital also.

The High School was four to five years old by the time Chhaya was in the seventh class. The hospital and the Block office had been there before the school was established. A branch of the Rural Bank had already been inaugurated a few days back. The local gentries were getting ready for setting up a college.

Chhaya's family was in no way extraordinaire. Her father Gananath realized that Mohangarh of his green days was no more there. He had some landed property. With the help of two labourers he used to sow the seeds and look up for tracing the signs of possible rain in the sky. At times when they failed to see any sign of rain, *poojas* were held with the cooperation of all. People got relieved when there was a shower. The rain god had been pleased with them. They brought the harvested paddy to the barn.

There was acute poverty in the village. As communication facility was there, many people left the village in search of jobs outside where they could earn their livelihood. The number of shops was increasing. The living condition was getting better as there was good business. Gananath had not understood the new wave properly. Even if he had assumed, there was no hope of his doing anything. Agricultural labourers were not available for it was wise for them to prefer working as helpers or drivers to working as labourers under the sun and slouching in the mud. Gananath's condition started becoming miserable. He often became unmindful under the pervading wave of indifferent coldness in the house. The signature of defeat had been clearly writ on his face. The torrent of time had drifted forward leaving him at a quiet bay. He would never be able to keep pace with that torrent. Thus sighs and pessimism made him incapable. During that phase of his life, Chhaya was studying in class seven.

As a student, she was mediocre. Of course, she was better at studies than her elder brother Tushar and younger brother Pravir. She went to school with endless enthusiasm, covered the new books and smelt their pages. As a mark of respect for learning, she touched the books with her head. While writing with the cheap pen, her fingers were ink-stained which she wiped off on her plaited long hair adorned with red ribbon. Ganesh and Saraswati poojas were held in the school. She, along with two others led the school prayer as she had a good voice.

It was only at the time of reading in the seventh class, the experience of credulous childhood- eating pickles, cheap lozenges, salted green mango slices and the play with friends and small sulkiness, everything was going to slip off. Many unknown things, confidential and prohibited, were there in the world she saw and knew.

Among all such things, one was like this- the teacher used to return the mathematics copy before the recess. Everyone got out of the class with the copy.

: "Is this copy yours?" The teacher asked Chhaya when she was alone.

: "Yes, Sir." Chhaya was left with no patience then. She repeatedly lookedat her friends walking along the road. She was in haste. On getting back the copy, she would join her friends in a single leap.

: "Take." The teacher handed over the copy. His remark was- "You haven't worked out all the sums, a few mistakes are there."

Getting back the copy was the primary thing for her. Never before was she alone with the teacher. Once the copy came to her hand, she would be there with her intimate group.

But she could not understand the teacher correctly. He had held Chhaya's copy in his left hand. His right hand stopped a while on Chhaya's head. His voice-"Your handwriting is good" was heard.

The teacher didn't say this to anyone else, not even to the wind. He intended it only for Chhaya's ear. Chhaya had never heard such a voice. She didn't realize why it was too low, slightly wavy and tinged with enough warmth.

While she extended her hand to get back the copy, the teacher's right hand was already caressing the sweaty neck and cheek of Chhaya. The hand moved downward.

While Chhaya stepped back frightened, the copy had already come to her hand.

Petrified she looked at the teacher's face for a moment. She was unable to believe the preceding moment's touch by the teacher. She seemed offended and confounded. But, looking at the teacher for a fraction of a second, she, as it were, could discover some things, quite obscure and beyond imagination. That touch was utterly new and strange. The teacher's face looked entirely different. She had never seen that face before. How could she know that the teacher's face would leave its place for the sake of such a different one?

Temporarily, Chhaya had clean forgotten that she would be there with her friends the moment she got back her copy. It was not sure what the teacher thought about looking at Chhaya's face. He said, "You are a good girl, no one can surpass you if you put in your efforts a little more."

While coming out of the classroom, Chhaya felt a thirst unseen before as if her throat had remained dry for years together. She walked at a slow pace for she had no urgent work. She also knew it for sure that she would stay separated from her friends for all time to come.

That very day, the seventh class student Chhaya had a hazy idea that the teacher's touch was something different although she could not comprehend its implication.

But at a later time, she understood that there was a unique language called 'touch'. It could express various and juxtaposed messages. 'Touch' could be such that it could never display the description of its total appeal.

Touch is an experience. Only the alert senses can understand its uniqueness instantly.

How could she as a small baby understand the touch of a mother's hand that massaged her body with the oil-turmeric paste? Even at a grown-up stage she could never understand the touch of a worried father's hand at her forehead and his loving words- "Still there is fever or how do you feel, my darling?"

She understood the touch of the friends at the time of being lost in playing holi and smearing the powdered colours.

Touch changes its meaning when someone's lusty touch in the crowd makes the body shrink. One takes it for a sign of danger and has to be alert despite the role of the light as the gatekeeper. There is still the touch of the lover on the lips, cheeks and neck. There is the touch of the husband amid the involuntary loneliness. Can a mother describe how it feels when the baby sleeps on the lap of immortality having the nipple of her breast in its mouth?

At times Chhaya reflected that the history of her life had been a history of different touches. She also thought how beautiful it wouldn't have been, if she was a cursed stone! At least, at the touch of someone's feet, she would have got up from the age-old sleep. Or had such feet come to her palms, washing which she would have got the touch of those feet on the pretext of welcoming to the boat like the boatman who washed Lord Rama's feet?

No such thing was predestined. Touch! It was poison. Touch! It was annihilation. Touch! It was death in life. Was she ever born to undergo all these and to be alienated losing all supports in the process? Such a life she lived and the people could never know what she was, a goddess or a monster.

All these experience would come at a later time. But, on that day during the recess, Chhaya was coming home idly. She didn't feel well at all. There was a tingling sensation whole over her body as if someone pricked a thousand pins. She felt like crying. Her body was surcharged with anger.

Everything from the school compound to the wet rice of the kitchen was lucid, beautiful and enjoyable. Touch was sweet and refreshing like the sandal paste. It was a close intimacy, a fragrant bond whereas; touch could also be tearful agony, a thorny affliction and the heartless bestiality over the mind and soul.

By the time she reached home, her father was washing his hands after taking lunch. Chhaya's returning home was a regular routine for which her father had given no attention to her except saying," You arrived late. I have finished my lunch. I was hungry."

His question was not about why she was late. However, he explained as to why there was the exception in eating together. Brother Tushar who was in class nine and younger brother Pravir reading in class four had not yet finished their lunch. All were in a good mood as if everything was enjoyable and pleasant.

There was a tremor in the thinking faculty of Chhaya. Would she tell her mother about what happened at school? She shrank. Would she to her friends-Sarala, Meena or Noopur?

What would she tell? How would she describe the matter? Or else should she caution them- "the teacher is a rogue, keep a distance from him"?

The time of remaining alone with a male was over so soon! Were they not secured and innocent? How could she tell? What would they think? Why did the teacher's hand move over Chhaya's body before it had bloomed?

The surprising thing was that the teacher could not look at Chhaya's face. Chhaya's face overcharged with anger and protest was observing him. She had decided she would shout and create a hue and cry in the classroom and the school campus in case the teacher did something like that. She would declare pointing her finger at the teacher, "The man is infested with a fatal virus. The virus comes down from his gaze and hand. His entire body is the centre of the virus."

For rest of the time in the Middle School, Chhaya had not encountered any unnatural touch; but at the time of getting herself admitted in the High School, she had been conscious about this. At times she was thrilled and lent her curious ears to the touch related episodes.

At the neighbour's the parents thrashed Bindu appa. Her elder brother gave the ultimatum to cut her throat. The incident taking place in their house somehow went public. People showered their family with reproof and contemptuous words. Bindu became a bad example for girls there. Groups of women gossiped about that. Chhaya knew another thing. Bindu appa was going to be an unmarried mother. She knew what M.T.P meant while she was at high school.

She also knew about Rasananda who, on returning home saw that his wife was not there. Rasananda who married only four months back came to know that his wife had eloped with her ex-lover. He did not want to get back his wife.

The fracture of Vaikuntha's leg didn't remain unknown for a day even. He would visit Narahari's house and won his confidence. Narahari had no knowledge that in the meanwhile Vaikuntha already had a clandestine relationship with his wife. He was caught. The doctor said Vaikuntha's condition would be severe if his legs were not amputated. Narahari sent back her wife to her father's house. He got married again and swore not to have any relation with any Vaikuntha sort of fellow.

These incidents were not that spicy as was the two-year-senior Jolly's affair. She had four lovers including one high school teacher. They were one another's competitors who applied different techniques to impress Jolly. She had the costliest wrist watch and pen. She also used wonderful perfumes. She would say that the slippers she used were not available in any nearby local market. It was not Chhaya alone, the other girls of the school stared with stunning amusement at Jolly's fashionable dress, her smart walk, her laughs and her efficiency in leadership.

They also had a craving in them for scented love letters written on blue paper having a picture of a rose bouquet on the left margin. On receipt of such letter, the blue colour of the paper, they wished, should expand like a sea. Waves of emotion and excitement were there. These waves under the full moon beams should be lofty and uncontrollable. The entire bouquet of roses would come up from the quiescent state. Its fresh petals would touch the face and the whole body to overwhelm with the mesmerizing aroma whispering, "We were blooming on our own before this, but lustre and the sweet smell remained preserved just to come to you only."

There were also small happenings concerning the girls including Chhaya, like someone passing with a nothing-has-happened look after making his body rub with that of a girl's; or caressing the hand unjustifiably while giving and taking the books and copies and pretending innocence but getting delighted internally.

As such, during the annual function of the school at the sudden power failure and before the alternative arrangement there was some uproar. Chhaya had felt amid the obscene utterance the heavy pressure of some unknown hand on her breast. By the time she stood up at the speed of lightning and before she shouted the light came back. She could not ascertain who that unrestrained boy was.

All these are the synonyms of touch. Darkness and solitude are needed for someone not only to touch her but to feel her body.

I LOVE YOU. It was written in English. All the eight letters were in the capital in green, red and blue colour. Chhaya discovered this paper inside a book. She could not know; could not guess even whose proclamation it had been. The message relating love was first of its kind for Chhaya to receive.

She was aware that her face had a silky beauty though she was slightly dark complexioned. With elongated slim eyebrows, her eyes looked dream-drenched and overwhelming. The most attractive part of her was her smile. That flashed her pearl white luminous teeth. Her cheeks would cooperate with her smile to hold its torrent, as it were, within two whirlpools.

'I love you'-proclaimed the piece of paper. There was no indication of the proclaimer's name. Such a large piece of paper was overwhelmingly surcharged only with an I-love-you proclamation. The hand that wrote it had forgotten to mention the writer's name. Was it a thing to forget? Poor fellow! He might not have the courage or might have been apprehensive of Chhaya's creating a hue and cry.

There was another piece of paper a few days after with a message in Odia- "You are in the pages of the book, on the shirt button, on the road, in the tree, and among the stars. You are here, there, everywhere. This world for me is full of Chhaya. I feel all the teachers are finishing their classes uttering the name of Chhaya only. The automobile horns, the chirping of the birds and the school bell- all of them are doling out the name of Chhaya. Chhaya! It's a hymn."

The letter without the sender's name had cut to size the power of thinking of Chhaya. The letter was a mad stream that drifted her. It was a violent tornado which lifted her away. Thus being floated and flown away was a non - existential state. She was there on the earth, yet in reality, she was not there. She was there in her intimate circle and was reading the literature book. Was she really reading? She was changing her school uniform at the corner of the house; but what was she doing indeed? How influential was the unique poetry written on that piece of paper! It was poetry in a real sense as if the language was created for writing this only.

Then for some days, she observed the faces of all coming to and going from the school. She was scanning their movements. What strange finger it was that held the magic pen! Could that finger accomplish something else like wringing the cloth, clearing the spider's web, holdingthe bicycle or eating even?

For days together the letter possessed her. And her expectant hand was turning the pages of the books and copies every day. Was there a letter like that anywhere? But there was none. She thought that she had not bought the books and the copies to read and write. What was their importance if letters were not found in every moment even though the writer disguised himself? The books and copies which she thought unnecessary burdens weighed heavy.

Only after a gap of almost ten days, there was a letter once again. There were awful concern and excitement with an uncontrollable palpitation. Chhaya's face was flushed and fevered. She read the letter confidentially as if she was doing some prohibited thing without the knowledge of anyone. The letter read like – "Why does the sleep break at night? Why do I think at present that Chhaya's breath should touch my chest at all the moments? Why do my hands remain extended to get Chhaya? The waters of the seven seas can never quench the thirst of my lips. They are waiting for Chhaya."

Chhaya thought as if she would go mad. The fire blazing in her mind and body would convert her to a heap of ash and the ash sitting on the zephyr's courier would go on searching for the writer of that letter. It would demand an answer from him as to why he filled in her so much of madness. One needed a great capacity to withstand and absorb it. She had none of that.

Chhaya became restless with acute anguish and a strange eagerness. She needed someone's strong embrace. That embrace should be so potent and trustworthy to hold the sky and the entire world within it. It should hold the present and the future and all activities of life as well.

The agony was unbearable, yet how desirable it was! How relishing too it was to have been crazy and to think of having been oblivious of the conscience! How enjoyable it was to have a restless bed and the urge of splitting the whole body! Further, how desirable it was to be mindful of making up and to be cheerful- for she was the object of attraction of one who did not write his name in the letter. How she, too, is not burnt by the invisible fire within! She was soliloquizing-"O you, reveal yourself, stop testing my nerves and patience. Stop there, and appear before me. I would come into the ring of your embrace gladly forsaking all. Extinguish the fire burning within me immediately and be calm. Bring my splitting and scattering thoughts to normalcy, help me to stand on."

The wait was endless. Nobody appeared. Chhaya,

impatient and restless, was ready to cry- O you reveal yourself, appear!

And then it was a small letter- "if you don't like my letters, tear and throw them near the flag post. I'll reckon that they have vexed you. Never shall I be so mad after that. I will tell myself that all dreams do not come true for a man like me".

Would she tear them? Was the writer apprehending it to be vexing? In that case, why should he not be called an idiot and stupid fellow? Why did the writer shrink and pitied himself thinking that the letters did not appeal to Chhaya very much? Whereas; Chhaya thought the very letter made her thirstier for more and more of it and this thirst got written of its own accord in her looks and behaviour. Could the writer not mark this much in her? Then what type of lover he was! What was the necessity of writing so many letters? What heart could he win with so much of mousey cowardice?

And the subject matter of the last letter was- "Stay on tomorrow in the classroom for a minute or two on some pretext after the school hour."

The next day was full of utter excitement and sky-kissing hopes. She kept her books and copies in order. She got irritated with herself for the work had been over so soon. She was the last to leave the class. She turned back as if something had been forgotten and started searching in the empty classroom for the thing that had never been left or lost. The desks and benches were vacant, even the smell of the sweat of the students was not there. The blackboard was speechless and there on it was the signature of the pencil chalk unrubbed off by the duster. Vacant and abandoned, odourless and speechless was the classroom. It was a lonely and unwanted world. All left therefore without giving a backward look.

She had been deserted and unwanted. All on a sudden she was frightened by the harrowing sound of the silent classroom. She was lost in utter grief. She would have cried almost under such agony.

She could not know whether she could normalize herself. She was surprised that Sarala, Meena, and Noopur had been standing at a distance of six or seven meters from the school building. They had been waiting for her only. She could not get a scope for explaining the delay as she wanted to get back the pen or pencil, she had left in the class.

: "Come, let's go. "There was sympathy in Meena's voice.

Pen or pencil- the search for the thing not lost- the curtain had fallen already as the drama was over. Chhaya had not known for whom was the halt on that stage for a minute or two. But the despair that buried the thrill and sweet palpitation had already made her speechless. She had no answer for Meena's empathy- 'come, let's go.'

Would anyone have come to you if you waited for a minute or two, or for a day or two, or even for a year or two? Sarala said with grief while along the road.

Chhaya was taken aback. There were a thousandpinpricks in her body and mind. She gave a nervous look at them. It was a mystery she knew but how could they also come to know?

: "We three had received such letters." Noopur revealed. She said further- "There was the advice in the fourth letter to stay on for a minute or two after the class had been over. Nobody had come."

: "Nobody had come." Meena repeated.

: In the third letter it was written- "To tear and throw it near the flag post if that was not liked."Sarala said.

: "These are the four letters I received." Noopur took out some pieces of paper and said, "The same letter in the same handwriting to three of us, your letter would not be different from those of ours."

: "We have tallied them," said Meena showing the letter she had. Sarala had started tearing the pieces of paper, Meena and Noopur followed her.

The four letters had already been heartless and taunting-garbage for Chhaya. She too tore that. But all the torn pieces of paper could not be under her feet. Scattered here and there they had lost their distinction and peculiarity.

Chhaya could never laugh the matter out. "Loafer and scoundrel," commented Noopur smilingly. "Rascal and a baseborn," Sarala gave vent to her fond slangs. Someone had sprinkled ink on her dress, and someone else had pinched her buttocks. Sarala took it for a joke and laughed.

: "If I found him, I would tell him- hey you damned wretch, why don't you show yourself if you dare writing letters? I would see how manly you are. I would see if you are a man. Why do you hide like a eunuch?" That was Meena's reaction. She always spoke out such words with all comfort. At times she also used obscene and vulgar slangs unhesitatingly.

That was the difference between them and Chhaya. Chhaya was more sensitive than they were. She was not comfortable with others.

She would be stunned to see the three mixing and talking freely with the boys. She wanted to be free and easy with others like snatching the pen from someone's hand while asking for it or putting the hand in some one's pocket charging at him "Why are you munching the mixture alone. Would you be the hero in the school drama? Hey, do you know how to deliver the dialogue"? Chhaya could not do like this. It was not proper to be so self-conscious.

Certain things are taken lightly, laughed out if necessary. She knew all that but could not adapt herself to all such things. She wanted her manners, movements, and idiosyncrasies not to attract others' attention. She could never conceive of the idea of becoming the cause for something. She could never give expression to her reactions. She could never raise her hand at the instance of the teacher although she knew the answer. She hummed the songs, possibly she could sing wonderfully to herself, but her voice became still and devoid of resonance. She shrank within herself. She could not assert her presence before others. She loved to lose her identity in the crowd.

The letter episode created in her a deep wound and she was confounded within. Anger and insult shook her inner being at the memory of the thrill and excitement created after getting the letters. She could not ask her friends about what had happened to them after they were aware of the joke the letter writer attempted at them.

Ostensibly they would say- reaction? Who would you give vent to your reaction if the person was not there? What we said at the time of tearing the letters was our reaction.

Was there any justification for giving so much importance to that incident? Should one be depressed if someone pulled the plait in the crowd or escaped whispering something obnoxious or even offered an ugly and offensive proposal calling your name? Who would you challenge, if there was none before you? Who would you confront with? Who would you be angry with if you were drenched in the rain; or if you stumbled on the way and your leg got into the mud? Was there any reason for getting angry? All such things would happen throughout the life. Life would be unbearable if your moods were off at all such trifles. The touchy one often suffered the most. Ordinary things appeared extraordinary. Its implication got exaggerated. Your mind and your way of looking at things made the mountain of a molehill. It was ordinary and insignificant.

Chhaya could get herself admitted in the college as the college was set up at Mohangarh in the year she passed her matriculation; otherwise, she would not have gone to the nearby college situated at a distance of 18 Kilometres.

Her elder brother had already opened a shop in the Market complex. It was a matter of solace that he was successful in that enterprise. His self-confidence had brought a change in his personality. He could know the demand and choice of the customers unmistakably. He often confessed of having the business knowledge only after he took to it. He would say- someone in me would ask me to do like that, to buy certain things in advance and to deal with such type of men in such manners. The magical conglomeration of all these is the little success of my business. Courage is necessary for that. You would lag behind if you hesitated to take risks. You would end up only in the midst of despair sighing all the while at the sight of others' prosperity.

Father Gananath had asked Tushar- "Are you doing any such things you oughtn't to?"

Tushar could not understand what it implied. He looked very smart. He had within him the patience and the tactics. His strong and sportive appearance gave such an impression. Tushar looked at his mother slicing the vegetable and Chhaya preparing to go to college. He looked at them as he could not know how to answer his father's question.

: "I could not get you," Tushar admitted. He asked a question instead- "Why should I do improper things?"

Gananath lingered as if he was searching for some clue. Tushar got aggrieved at his father's words. He asked, "I don't know why you entertained the idea that I was doing improper things?"

: "You might be cheating the customers." The father was bold and straight. He had not finished.

: "Perchance, you stocked duplicate things." Pausing for a moment, he said, "I don't suspect you, I just warn you."

: "I want to stabilize myself in business." There was amazing boldness in what he said. "I don't want to stop there; I want to march ahead. If I take to cheating and unfair means, how long shall I be in this business?" He gave a picture of his future through this question.

Gananath did not say anything further. After he had left the place, an intensely hurt Tushar told Chhaya, "I was not honest in studies and at examinations. I admit that. Does it mean I'll be dishonest in business also? I didn't like that." He decried.

: "So you took his words this way?" Tushar's mother defended her husband and said, "He told it for your good whereas you take it to your heart."

He did not seem to have been consoled. He said, "The books and copies weighed heavily on me; I was almost bending myself to manage the load. But you see- heavy bags and cartoons would be loaded on the carrier; I lift them with zest. I have an interest in that. I give a loving touch to my commodities in my shop. My shop is the temple of goddess Laxmi. Should I stock duplicate things there to cheat the customers and pollute the temple? How strange! What nonsense!"

: "Listen." Chhaya said adding some words of praise- "You have achieved success in business within a very short time. Since father's confidence in your capability is shaky, he could not believe it so easily."

Tushar did not look satisfied. He said, "If a customer left something- may be the spectacles or the umbrella, I would find out the owner to hand over the thing. If anyone tried to cheat me, I would cut him to size in my way."

: "My way- What do you mean by that?" Chhaya asked.

: "I try to make such type of men ashamed without any grudge. Tushar was telling about some business techniques. He continued, "I give them the idea that they were doing something wrong inadvertently. They had no deliberate design to deceive me."

There was a rapid change in Tushar's personality. He was no more the helpless, pathetic and reticent boy of the School days. He was also sure of his success in the competition in his sphere. He was gentle in his behaviour. Nonetheless, a strong determination and stubbornness made some room in him. He would take decisions with future prospects in mind and never bothered to slow down for the competitor lagging behind. There was no place of sentiments in these matters. He regarded business as a battlefield. If won, you had the kingdom. If lost, there would be no one at your back.

The market was expanding. Therefore, the landed property of Gananath had become as valuable as gold. Tushar had already planned for a three-roomed house, but immediate telephone connection and a motorbike had become urgent necessities.

His view about his younger brother was- "Let him pass the matriculation first. I'll ask him what he would do- whether to go to college or to assist me in the business. I have marked him having an interest in the business. After all, what benefit is there whiling away the time with some loafers, falling in after the girls or creating undesirable problems in the college and market?"

: "Why do you say so?" Chhaya protested. The college is there at hand. Let him read there for some years. If he passed anyway, would he not have the prestige of a graduate? She tried to convince.

: "What would he do having a degree like that?" Tushar was pessimistic. He cannot be an officer, what would he do with that degree, would it feed him? What do you say Pravir- will you continue your studies or do business with me?"

Before Pravir had said anything, Chhaya replied- "What would he say? For the time being, you are more than enough for the business. He would read in the college."

While mulling over to or not to say, Tushar blurted- "Hun, College!" He derided. He said, "You forbade me, otherwise I would have finished the two who used to harass you by sending letters and passing ugly comments in the street. Bloody, studying in the college! See the behaviour of the college students. What will Pravir do acquiring such behaviour?"

Chhaya shrank. She had nothing to argue further in favour of the college. Only Noopur from among her friends was reading in a college staying at her uncle's. She had revealed a number of times that she was not feeling comfortable there anymore. Where was the pleasure staying there when people at the uncle's took her for a burden? Meena got plucked and denied to do exercise with the books any more. Sarala got the tailoring training after passing the supplementary examination. She said that she got satisfaction out of it as she got a good number of orders. In the meanwhile, she thought of Chandan Sir who had met her brother Tushar very recently.

: "I had been to your brother's shop yesterday." Seizing an opportunity, he said. His certificate was like this- "Very smart, very well behaved! He became more courteous in knowing me as a lecturer. He said, "My sister Chhaya is reading here."

Prof. Chandan paused for a while and marked that Chhaya waited with happy and eager ears to listen to something more. He beamed with a broad smile. Possibly he felt encouraged. He said, "I told him, I know Chhaya- that calm, attentive, patient girl with a wonderful smile. No other name would have been befitting for her."

Chhaya felt a warm wave sweeping within. Not for once but for time and again this wave rose in her. As if it would overwhelm her mortal frame! Once again the enchanting language! Once again, the thrill and shivering! Once again, the feeling of breathless flight and floating! Unlike the previous occasion, these words weren't written in a letter; the words emerged directly from the mouth; andthe person expressing his opinion was right in front of her. He was real.

Chhaya could not say anything. Perhaps no one was saying anything to her, nor was she listening to anything. Only was she feeling the warmth of a clasping embrace. It seemed to her that she was in the ring of Chandan's embrace placing her face on his chest. She felt his hand moving across her back and cheeks. That was not an impatient hand; as it were, it had the eternity under its control for moving across Chhaya's entire body.

Chhaya desired that at that time. Chandan's face spoke of trust. He wanted to tell more and more but did not feel its necessity as Chhaya had known what he did not say.

She only kept on gazing at Chandan's face. She was not conscious that her lips were throbbing slightly. And even in that situation,silky drowsiness was descending on her eyes.

: "I know you are so nice." Chandan said in a whisper.

The meeting was unexpected. After the letter episode at the school, Chhaya kept herself at a safe distance from such probable encounters. But all on a sudden Chandan stunned her. Such dialogues come up only after the acquaintance was old and intimate. Chandan's talk was unexpectedly abrupt.

The remark of the teacher when she was in class seven was- "You are a good girl." He had to say that as a penance for his conduct. Such butter-up was necessary to balmify wounded Chhaya, but that had no impact on her. The present situation was something different. She had been experienced and had known that touch meant expression. She had been quite adept at understanding and assessing the meaning and magnitude of the language spoken.

Would she ask in what sense she was 'very good'? She had no courage for that. Nonetheless; she enjoyed that remark. Again she looked at Chandan and walked past giving a smile along with an impression that she acknowledged the admiration with pleasure. But she stopped after taking eight or ten steps.

She stooped and looked back on a pretext that the slipper gave some problem. Standing at a distance,Chandan kept gazing at her with utmost delight. She felt exalted and fulfilled when she marked that Chandan had been waving his right hand to bid goodbye to her in such a manner that no one could see him.

This thrilling fitfulness was new. The world had not seemed so loving and beautiful hereto before. So lyrical and graceful! And everything in the world had come to a halt. None was there in the wide wide world. There was only the state of being lost- the redemption in a clasp of embrace through total surrender. The comment gifted for the first time- 'You are very good' had metamorphosed into a symphony. That symphony was created only for Chhaya to faint while listening to it with rapt ecstasy.

That night at the dining table she said to Tushar- "What way did you entice Professor Chandan? He is full of praise for you-you are very smart, and your behaviour is very wonderful, etc., etc."

Tushar was elated.

In fact, Chhaya was telling him to please him. She tried to create a favourable impression in him towards Chandan. He asked, "Did he praise me? Wow! But I should praise him. He speaks so nicely! He seems to be a very learned person."

He was telling with overflowing pleasure that he knew the basic principles of business. Chhaya could not see why she was telling such lies. Her question was- "Basic principles of business! Where and how did you learn those?"

Tushar looked contented and fulfilled. In a trance, he said, "Do you think that there is no formula and technique in business? They are there. Could a house filled with commodities be a shop and a man sitting there would be called a shopkeeper, a businessman? Taking a pause, he said, "Professor Chandan is a good man. No, not me alone, some others have the same opinion as mine."

: "He teaches well." She added and became a little confounded within.

Rest of the time was the time for humming and ruminating. Chhaya felt very light. She felt an ant in her trousers; when would the daybreak? Would the night end! What would she tell Prof. Chandan in the boisterous college atmosphere?

Amid the gathering and movement of students, a moment could be stolen. At the checking of the copies of a small tutorial group, Chhaya's was the last. Chandan asked, "Have you written anything in the copy?"

: Yes, Sir, here it is!" Chhaya bent forward. She could not understand the question properly.

: "Where are the letters?" Chandan looked at innocent Chhaya's face and said, "I only see your face in each of the letters. This time he said holding her hand, "Had you written or drawn your picture with this hand?"

In a twinkle of an eye, Chhaya had come to a free state beyond her control. The heat of her body found no outlet in her breath to escape. Droplets of sweats accumulated on her face. Chandan put the *chunri* that slipped off her shoulder back in its right place. He went out without checking the copy. Trying to hold herself, Chhaya also came out of the classroom.

What was the future of the passion that had obsessed her? Chhaya could find no anchor, no commitment for that. The seventh class experience lacked that touch. The present touch was desirable and finally approved. She cherished the touch of Chandan. She wished to be locked in his embrace until she lost her consciousness. There was madness in her for grabbing that moment. That moment was not the total life! She could whiff out the time and all other needs of life for the sake of getting that cherished moment. She would want to dissolve herself in a trice like that.

She did not give any importance to the experience concerning the anonymous letter at school. She argued that the letter was unreal and its writer non-existent. This time, Prof. Chandan was real and human. She saw him, listened to him and had the actual feel of him. She wanted his deep intimacy. He would rack his brains for being Chhaya-minded. She needed that. She would keep him in her possession. He could never imagine what might happen to his poor world without Chhaya. He could never think of the flying butterfly, the cheer of the blossoming flowers, the murmur of the brook or the careless chirping of the birds without the presence of Chhaya. He would think like that, and that would be the priceless achievement of Chhaya.

Along the entire road, she caressed her right hand and got the touch of a warm hand. It was here, here and here! She lifted the caressed hand to her nose, kept it on the lips. She apprehended that the intensity of the touch would diminish if she washed the hand or if it came with the contact of dust and wind.

It was almost one o'clock by the time she reached home. There was still some time left for lunch. She changed her dress and washed up against her will. She consoled herself that it was not the last touch. She saw herself in the mirror as if for the first time. While seeing herself, she became dreamy; she smiled and sulked and wrinkled the brows. There was a surprise; there was a pleasure. All her postures looked unique. Had anyone done like that before her to create a different emotion and see its reflection?

Could they look so attractive?

: "Would you like to have your lunch now? You must be feeling hungry." Her mother asked standing at the door.

: "No. I am not hungry. Let them come. We'll eat together."

Her mother was still capable. Before Tushar had taken to business, the house seemed very dull. The parents also looked hopelessly helpless. But after the improvement in their condition, her mother seemed like enjoying life. Tushar and Pravir had enthusiasm for their work. They had the realisation that the unseen fate cooperates with hard work to yield a good result.

The road infront of the house was not black-topped. Mohangarh was a big village. This house of Gananath was in the street.

The market that was coming up was to the right of this road. It had expanded almost up to Gananath's house. Chhaya came out of the house to go to College situated to the left of the road. It was only a twenty minutes' easy walk from her home. Within four years many a building had been constructed. The construction work was still going on.

All the rooms of the College- large and small were under lock and key. The cycle-stand near the gate after the college hours would lay dumb and lifeless. Chhaya had heard that this small world lay under the care of two night-watchers.

Prof. Chandan put up with some other persons in a mess on rent. All of them were college teachers. They enjoyed prestige, position, and respect in the small town like Mohangarh. They were conspicuous while on the road, shopping or at any discussion anywhere. The people in the town would listen to them with interest and rapt attention.

The shopkeepers would prefer attending them to other customers. One would feel fortunate to be acquainted with them. No one would think of having any doubt over their erudition or their specialization in other fields.

All of a sudden on a Sunday Chhaya heard, "Please come in. We would be sorry if you feel shy here in our house. You would have whatever simple food we have like wet rice and cooked leafy vegetables."

Just fifteen minutes back Chhaya had shampooed her head as she would do on every Sunday. She had not combed her hair till then. She was in an old faded dress.

She stopped at the door while coming out in a hurry from under the fan to see who her brother had called in. She could not believe her eyes. A pleasant surprise! She could never express its wild sharpness. Her eyes dazed. She was obliged. She felt like changing into a sea with such an unexpected wave of experience and so unbound a joy. The high tides of feelings and excitement that rose in her were searching for an outlet; without getting it, they broke blindfold on the beach of her body. She would reject the saying at that very moment that daydreams never come true.

Prof. Chandan stood at the centre of the courtyard. He looked shy and confounded. His smiling lips looked pitiable.

Mother stood on the kitchen corridor with a spatula in her hand. Tushar introduced him: "Mother, this is Prof. Chandan who teaches our Chhaya in the College. He had come to my shop for some pickles, *papad,* and biscuits."

The cook of his mess left for his village on getting the news about his father's illness. Sir would have cooked for himself. I have called him. You arrange for his lunch here. I will take him back on my return after an hour or two.

Her mother pulled her veil as a mark of respect. She

did not know as to how such unexpected guests were treated. Nonetheless, she saluted him. Looking confounded she said, "Where has Chhaya gone?" And by and by, she said as if discovering her, "Oh, there she stands!" She said to Chhaya, "Take your teacher into the room; I've some work left here."

Chhaya also greeted him in the same spell-bound state. Her mother went to the kitchen. Tushar's bike started for the market.

No room of that house was earmarked as the drawing room. The space called the passage hall accommodated Tushar's motorcycle, Pravir's cycle, and the shoes and slippers. Two chairs along with a bench lay there. The visitors would sit there and talk. Beyond this room, there was the courtyard in front of which were three bedrooms. The kitchen was to its right.

Chandan stood under the fan in Chhaya's room. The room had in it a bed along with a chair, a table, and a rack. There were books, copies and some stickers of the pictures of gods and goddesses.

Chhaya had withdrawn her gaze from Chandan's face. Although he saw her, he did not want to say anything. Chhaya apprehended that she would melt and become a non-entity in the twinkle of an eye.

: "Sir, a cup of tea if you like?" She spoke with her voice quivering. Drenched in sweat, she asked in a whisper, "What are you thinking so deeply?"

: "I haven't come here for tea or lunch, have I?" Chandan, who was going to be almost speechless, said licking his lips, "I told him that I was going to cook for me. I was sure, the trick would work, and it did. See, I'm here before you, being invited by your brother." He said in a quivering warm voice, "I LOVE YOU!"

Chhaya didn't know how to respond to what Chandan

had said. The closing sound of the kitchen door made Chhaya conscious before anything adventurous happened. She came out to the corridor. Her mother said, "Going to bring some coriander leaves from the garden. Would your teacher like to have some *sorbet* or tea? Take care of him until I finish cooking."

Chhaya came back into the room again. Subsequently, she felt the movement of Chandan's finger through her hair. She felt the touch of his fervid breath on her neck and the touch of his impassioned lips on hers. All these spoke the language of touch. All blood cells all over her body turned wild and out of tune. The pain in pleasure was so very unbearable that Chhaya despite all her efforts could not check a small cry of alarm. That utterance, as it were, was a gift to Chandan before her sense and feeling had been numbed.

During the subsequent Sundays, her mother felt comfortable with Chandan. It was not Chhaya's problem relating to study matters that she highlighted on; she commented primarily upon her remarkable efficiency in house-management. She had an excellent hand at cooking. That day she had cooked with pleasure all the items that Chandan relished. She had never seen such sense of responsibility with anyone. She kept herself awake if anybody fell ill. She would remind him the medicine time. She had such a soft and sympathetic heart that she could never tolerate anyone's suffering. The sweater you see there has been knit by her, she said.

Not only Chhaya's mother but also Gananath and Tushar felt encouraged by what Chandan said in Chhaya's praise: "She was very quiet and restrained at the college. Her behaviour pleased everyone. She would listen to the lectures with rapt attention. She had an appreciable handwriting. It was sure that she would do well in the examination. If I got time, I would come to help her with her studies."

The affair lasted for five to six months. Chandan would come to their house. The family felt fortunate for that. But it appeared that there lacked something in their treatment to him despite all care and keenness. Chandan, five feet six inches tall was of medium built. He could be called handsome. He appeared very innocent and inexperienced. But Chhaya knew what much of cleverness and potent warmth had been lurking behind the seeming semblance of indifferent disinterestedness.

Chandan was very intelligent, possibly sly. He got lost somewhere after Chhaya's B.A. Exams were over. It was not known to Chhaya how the college classrooms and the mess pined for him. Because it was beyond her imagination that Chandan had any relation with any person or thing of the world save her.She would not fathom the possibility of such a relationship. However, Mohangarh did not see him anymore. From some mysterious source Chhaya got the information that Chandan had got a good job.

Four years at college slipped off in no time. Chhaya had to go nowhere after that. No Ganesh or Saraswati puja would be there for her anymore. Annual function of the college, participation in the chorus, who bought how many *rakhis*, which girl had how many lovers and which girl was caught red-handed in objectionable postures with which capable nonstudent- among all these was the encounter with Chandan Sir, smiling and complimenting, "This *kameej* suits well on you" in an inaudible undertone. Wow! With what enthusiasm they gossiped!

Everything was over. Time deserted her at such a

point that she did not know how to go ahead. If she went ahead, which goal would she reach? She was not sure. That was the terrible feeling of being left alone, that too in a world without Chandan, a fainting feeling! There was eternal and infinite emptiness; Chhaya also felt how meaningless her life had become and how motionless it was without the least stir or vibration!

Chandan! There was a constant hum of a wailing within and without her. 'Where are you? Come here, come for once at least. I yearn for a meeting with you. Do you think I would ask you for something and you would fail to fulfil my demands? And I would enjoy your helplessness? Why should I ask you for something? All that I have got had come down from you before I asked for it.

There had been no open discussion at home regarding Chandan's absence. His whereabouts were not known nor was there any interest in others to know about him. Of course, a picture of diffidence was there with everyone. Chhaya thought that everyone had been daydreaming about Chandan Sir. She too had become extra ambitious. Was she worthy of getting Chandan Sir?

She went to college and said an official in the office that some books of Prof. Chandan were there with her. The address was necessary to send the books. She got the address. She would write in a trembling hand. And she did not know what she wrote exactly. There would be no reply to her letter. She continued writing letters. While waiting for an answer, the intimation letter for admission into C.T training programme reached her.

Oh, what a great relief the letter brought! Over the last few days, Chhaya had the feeling that the energy and zest in her were exhausting. Despair gave fury a way to intensify. Since she was betrayed, an acute sense of diffidence overpowered her, turning her devoid of self-confidence. At this juncture,she received such a letter. This indicated the course she would take and prepare herself to reach the destination.

She was astonished to see all the members of the family welcome the message. She had the apprehension that there might be some opposition to that service. Her friends were getting ready for family life; some of them had already been mothers.

A conservative woman like her mother also beamed at this and said, "Why wouldn't father agree? I would take that responsibility. He would give his consent but where and how would you put up yourself? Would you be able to stay away from home? You used to feel a fish out of water in any relative's house after staying there for a day or two."

: "See, stop that nonsense," Tushar said in a threatening voice. He spoke in favour of Chhaya, "She will stay in the hostel like all other girls. She has grown up. She is a graduate and can take care of her."

Pravir helped her in matters of admission and hostel accommodation. While taking leave of her, he said, "Appa, you will be at a distance of a hundred kilometers from home, and you will have to change two buses for going and coming to and from home. You write if you want something. Pending all other things, I will rush to you the moment I receive your message. You stay and have the hostel food with pleasure. Mix with others cautiously. Make sure that you don't hurl yourself into unnecessary troubles."

He indicated at the frustrated relation with Prof. Chandan. Pravir was the younger of the two. He who once was poor at studies had become clever in the meanwhile. He was giving final shape to his plan of business expansion. His confidence was growing like that of Tushar.

The asbestos roofed long building was the hostel. The walls were dull and faded with spider's web here and there. Some names had been written with chalk pencil on the door and window panels. The beds and the tables were very old. It was a four-seated room. On one side there was the common-toilet, and the kitchen and the dining hall stood on the other. Her trunk and bedding material were still on the cot. She gave a listless passive look on the three other beds spread already and over the boarders moving along the corridor. She heard boisterous giggling, loud chit chatting, argument and fragments of songs.

Heaving a sigh, she came up to spread the bed. It was, as it were, she was opening the gate of her future. For the time being, she would enjoy the ghee and fried rice her mother had packed. Brother Tushar had bought her a new torchlight and handed over enough money. She would go to the dining hall from that evening. She would be with her roommates.

THREE

The wound, fresh and possibly to remain ever new, was burning. The best part of her being lay half dead. Chhaya had no such hope that it would resurrect and that she'd ever be able to start enjoying life and the world again. Everything had changed its significance after the break down of her relationship with Prof. Chandan. She had already begun to see everything, every language, every touch and every beckoning from a modified perspective.

Passion! It needed no analysis. She could not think about its repercussions. The disposition would govern the thoughts and actions. Only that was certain and true. She would reflect like this.

A newly developed consciousness in her discriminated the good from bad, proper from improper and the essential from trifle. The horizon of truth and reality was expanding. Chhaya looked at herself against that backdrop. Some incidents seemed childish and irresponsible and absurd due to lack of knowledge about the peril and reality. The thoughts — was she that foolish and ludicrous or particularly, what for the relation with Prof. Chandan developed or even the question— was there any commitment in that confounded her.

Yes, of course! A voice within her peeped out and asserted itself. There were a few rare moments. They would remain as part of her experience. There were some unique touches also. She felt themtill that day. Perhaps the feeling would be there for all time to come. The pressure on the entire body, the warm breath and the impassioned lips- the touch and the moment- all were real. Not only she but he too needed it. They were gratifying each other. There were a belief and confidence that both the moment and the touch had a future. Such a hope came later; there were only the moments and the excitement for the touch. Just that was desirable, nothing more.

That time she could never say, "I LOVE YOU." But Chandan could. Maybe, at that time Chhaya had engrossed his impassioned self. Chandan too was in search of that moment and touch which he availed from Chhaya. He left the place. Ostensibly, no more did Chhaya remain the only necessity for him. Okay, if it didn't happen like that; she could wish him in the least- "Wish you all the best."

She would mix with many in the hostel. Many of them were senior to her in age; married too. They were in jobs in different schools. Chhaya showed them due respect. She was polite and obedient and helped them in small things too.

However, a series of incidents like Tushar's marriage, construction of a new building before that and the preparation for another storey took place in a very short span of time. That too, all of them were good. Pravir had already started his new business and had bought a motorcycle.

Gananath said cautioning his two sons, "Both of you tell me, giving serious thought on the matter, whether you will stay together or separately. In pen and paper, I have distributed the landed property. If you stay together, you won't do anything secretly. You will consider everything together. Both of you must discuss things and take decision only after that. Each of you will have to contribute equally to household expenses."

Both of them were staying together, and as they said, there was no problem whatsoever.

Chhaya had a small role in selecting her sister-in-law. She had been to three or four places for the purpose. However, Tushar was at full liberty to assert his choice.

The other good thing was that she did not have to sit at home for many days after the training. Chhaya got an appointment as an assistant teacher in a Middle English School situated at a distance of twenty Kilometres from Mohangarh.

The entire family felt ecstatic. There was a festive mood in the family. They had not experienced such abundance of pleasure on the occasion of the inauguration of the new house. Tushar saw the appointment letter and tried to read it. He was able to figure out two things from that. The first one was by what date she was to join and the second the name of the school.

He placed both the hands of Chhaya on his palms and kissed them. Never before had he looked so happy and contented. Then it was Pravir. He said, "Appa, give me the order, I'm ready to carry out whatever you ask me to do. Is there anything I should bring for you?"

The Mother stood leaning against a pillar. Gananath sat on the veranda. He looked overwhelmed and grateful to God. At least, at that moment, everything appeared accomplished. At least for the time being they had nothing more to pray for. All the three children had grown capable. They needed no support. They would stand on their own feet with pride. They would defend themselves. That was no less an achievement for the parents.

: "All of you have gone crazy with happiness," Gananath said expressing concern. The cause of his concern was due to the distance of the school from home and the lack of good road communication. "First, think about what she would do?"

Gananath's dismay and concern could not subdue the jubilant mood. "I would buy a motorbike for appa to commute to and fro the school; I'd train her how to ride it," said vainglorious Pravir.

: "I would go to the office of the D.I or C.I," gave out Tushar. He added, "Let's see if I can do anything. There would have been nothing to worry if she had been posted in a school having a good road communication, no matter how distant it was."

He came to realize that these considerations had been demoralizing Chhaya. Patting on the back of his younger sister, he started boosting her, "Listen, you have become a school teacher; it's not a small thing. You will teach and control the students; if necessary, you will cane them." Overcharged with surprise, he stopped on imagining the role of Chhaya as a teacher.

He confessed, "I can't believe that the little Chhaya of yesteryears is now a teacher. Chhaya, just tell us what you want; Pravir and I would get that for you in no time."

: "I think of joining tomorrow," said Chhaya and continued, "I will see the school; there would be no problem if they arrange for my accommodation. Pravir, could you help me tomorrow in this regard?"

: "What makes you hesitate to ask this," Pravir protested. He said, "Give me the order what I am to do for you. At what time tomorrow should we start; at nine or ten?"

Such a time entertains no grudge on anyone nor is

there any sense of lacking anything due to the pleasure of achieving something. Chhaya was grateful to her propitious fortune. She was obliged to the thirty-three-million gods. Her eyes flooded with tears when she stood in front of the deities. She said, "These tears of gratitude are the bouquets for you, they are the offerings, they are the lamps and the gongs of bells and chanting of your name."

She could not sleep for the whole night. The appointment letter was the answer to all her past failures and frustrations. That was the balm on all her sufferings, big and small. No dry desert was in the offing nor was there any undulated rough realm. Everything appeared green and promising. A different chapter of life was going to begin.

But Chhaya's enthusiasm receded proportionately with the motorcycle advancing. It was not a road in its proper sense; it was rather a slightly wide separator amid the fields on its either sides. The so-called road, as it were, obstructed the pedestrians and even the cattle. That was a great challenge to any driver. That ran along some villages as if it was determined to cross all of them. Did this road run toward the particular school? Chhaya wasn't sure. Where was she heading to- to the school or to the place of banishment?

Pravir stopped the motorcycle at a square where there were three or four small shops. He said, "Let me find out how far the school is."

He looked exhausted, a little vexed too. Of course, he was astonished how the distance had not been covered despite his biking for hours together.

He felt somewhat relieved as the compound of the Middle School was visible from that place. All the shopkeepers and the customers looked at them. They stared at them with curiosity just as one does on seeing unexpected persons. On seeing a tea shop, Pravir asked if she would like to have some.

By that time Chhaya had grown extremely worried. She knew it was not possible for her to relish the taste of tea or anything else for that matter. She had some water, and by and by, she had two sips of the hot liquid with a smoky smell which had no semblance of tea. Pravir also could not relish that thing called tea. He gave out a faint smile. Switching on the motorcycle engine, he asked her to sit on.

The gate they arrived at was the gate of the Middle School. Like the tattered apparel of a poor man, the hedge was torn and disconnected. Yonder the entrance was a long tile-roofed house. It was the school. Including comparatively two bigger rooms, there were three rooms. The smallest was the office. The noise of the children insome room reached the road. Perhaps, the teacher was not there. The school bell hung from the wooden beam of the corridor.

The small house adjacent to the school building was abandoned. It was dilapidated. Chhaya got to know later that students used to come from far off places to read here, as it had a reputation. They stayed in that house which functioned as a hostel. It's not known why the school lost its reputation. Perhaps private Middle Schools came up in nearby villages changing the preference of the students.

The school building was also in bad condition with mossy walls and miserable cement floor that posed great danger to the feet that trod on it. Wild growth of vegetation filled the campus. The *Taraat* tree was sick. There were some China rose plants also. While they stepped on to the corridor, the two sleeping dogs raising their heads for a moment looked indifferently at them and relapsed into sleep.

He must have been the Headmaster, who in Dhoti and kameez came out of the classroom.

After the introduction by Pravir, they sat together in the office granting absolute freedom to the children.

"There is no problem in your joining as the school has already received the letter," the Head Master said. He said further that the other assistant teacher was on leave. It would be better if Chhaya took the classes soon. The studies of students were getting affected for different reasons, of which he did not mention any. His house was three Kilometres away from the school. He commuted to and fro by his bicycle. He had been there in that school for the last fifteen years. The assistant teacher had joined there two years back. His house was at a distance of five kilometers. The peon who belonged to that village had become old and would retire after a year. With his retirement, the post of the peon would be abolished.

Where would Chhaya put up herself? The Headmaster looked worried and sympathetic. He said, "Seven or eight years back, a lady teacher had been posted here. She stayed as a paying guest in someone's house. She had to cook for herself as there was some problem. The problems made her so disgusted that she got herself transferred to a school near her village just after a year of her joining here. I am afraid Chhaya madam might be in troubles for some days."

The school peon reached there at that time and heard everything. Giving her some hope he said, "I would arrange for the accommodation of this daughter in a good family." Giving a glance at the Headmaster, he continued, "It is in the house of Atanu, the Panchayat Secretary. It will be suitable."

They were a bit relieved to have heard that. Pravir

did not wish to waste any more time. Chhaya would wait in the school for some time. The Headmaster suggested that it would be better to spend the time with the students in a classroom than in the office. Pravir took the peon with him and rode into the village.

Chhaya was tired and hungry. The matters regarding her lodging had made her worried and lost. But, the suggestion of going to a class made her spirited. She stood smiling in the classroom. The students looked at her with eager and curious eyes. Possibly, that was the welcome note for Chhaya. The language of silence indicated the cordial acceptance. Once again, she looked at the students giving a hint that she would derive pleasure and satisfaction in teaching them. Perhaps, her perseverance had in view the only goal of teaching them. The worry relating to the twenty-km-long-no-go road and the difficulty due to unavailability of accommodation remained pending. No problem whatsoever stood before her desire of getting success and satisfaction. She stood in the classroom and said that it was their Mathematics period. She asked whether they had brought the books and asked them to raise their hands if they had.

And many hands were there before her. That was the reaction to her first instruction. It was an involuntary action- a host of dazzling 'yes we have' appeared on their shoulders. Only three girls with oil soaked plaits and red ribbons sat on a bench together in class seven. Chhaya saw them and thought about what sort of behaviour the teacher showed there while correcting their books. She reconstructed her bygone school days. Still, after so long a time she felt an indistinct wave in her body. What had her teacher seen in her that he became so eager to explore her body?

Had her body such attractions? Possibly! Wasn't she

comparatively more attractive than others when she was in class seven?

Pravir returned almost after one hour. Although there wasn't the trace of total despair, he seemed not that satisfied. His face showed that he had not been unsuccessful. He would take Chhaya to show the house.

Atanu, the Panchayat Secretary, said, "Our family is the first in the village in using the *barapalli* latrine. Madam may use that as well as the bathroom. If she liked, she would have her meals with us or else she could cook for herself in the room at the end of the veranda."

Theirs was a four-roomed neat house with a broad courtyard having a compound wall. The room which was to be given to Chhaya, though not connected with the house was not entirely disconnected. Non-veg. items were prohibited there.

Atanu said, "During father's time different types of holy men used to come to our house. This house and the small kitchen had been constructed keeping their requirements in view. They would not touch the food cooked in our house. Father left for the other world a year ago. The saints and holy men are not coming anymore. We were embarrassed during their stay here. We had to be very careful about respecting their austere ways.

: "Manageable!" she said to herself. She said, "I would stay here if you have no problem."

Pravir looked relieved. He said, "Atanu babu, the other matters regarding my appa's stay here..."

He could not finish the sentence. Atanu said with a smile, "I know what matter you want to speak about. Number one-we won't take any rent for this house, two- if madam took her food with us, the payment towards that will be decided later. Number three- we have two children and my sister, who has married in this village, also has two children. All of them are reading in this school. Madam has to teach them. What do you say?" The question was intended for Chhaya.

There had been no power supply to this village twenty-five years ago. The poles were erected only. Towards the end of this year, they would be connected with wires, and there would be power supply from the beginning of the next year. It was a different matter to what extent the people believed or disbelieved such announcements.

The next day, Chhaya reached the new place by half past nine in the morning. She had brought with her a small bed, a small suitcase, and a mini-transistor radio. Atanu was to arrange a pitcher, a mug and a bucket. All these were arranged soon after she had reached there.

Despite his protest, Pravir took two pancakes with some veg-stew at Atanu's. As he had no other work, he returned.

After a minute or two, Chhaya stood in her room. She was ready to go to school. She had taken care so as not to look gaudy or special. Therefore, there was no sharpness either in the colour of her saree or in the facial make- up. She had tried to avoid the things attracting others' attention.

While she stood like that, she felt anxious and uncertain. But, at least, the quick and satisfactory arrangement of everything had created enough self-confidence and mental strength in her. Taking food with the family made her feel light and free of botheration. In fact, she had been grateful to the family. Though Atanu's wife was not highly educated, she had established herself as an experienced housewife in the meanwhile. She created an impression in Chhaya that she could take her care and could love her. This made Chhaya safe.

She came out of the room to go to the school. Would she keep her room under lock? She changed her decision for nobody would accept that. She saw Atanu's wife sitting there and separating something from the winnowing fan mindfully.

: "*Vouja,* I'm going to school. Where are the children? We would go together." She addressed her as vouja for the first time.

: "They?" She had been overwhelmed with the address. "They have left already." Pausing for a moment, she said, "Come during the recess; that is our lunch time."

: "O sure." With a cordial smile, she said, "Should I go without food when the vouja was at home?"

Chhaya had a happy time. She would finish all daily chores by seven in the morning every day as she had to tutor four children for two hours. Then she would get ready for the school. After the school hour, despite all deterrence, she would assist the sister-in-law in the kitchen keeping an eye on the children at the same time. The children would go to bed first after having dinner. The rest had dinner approximately at ten o' clock.

Sometimes there would be some deviation from that schedule due to Abhinna, Atanu's younger brother. Nobody knew it exactly where he went and what sort of politics he practiced. He was not very conscious of his dress also. Most of the time his hair would be dry and unkempt and his face bearded. He would talk in a slightly loud voice and give an idea of not caring anyone in the world.

He saw Chhaya. He questioned Atanu about who she was and why she was there. He would not say anything after hearing what Atanu had to say nor would he say anything objecting to her stay there.

Her staying there or leaving the place would not

matter much to him. In fact, he gave a distant and indifferent glance at her like one gives at a stranger in a crowd. He gave no importance to her presence there. He could not manage to pass the matriculation despite making three attempts. "He would usually laze around, but once he did something mindfully, he would simply excel. No one would be at par with him." Vouja told her in a depressed tone. She perhaps wanted Abhinna to change his lifestyle and to mind the work at home. He was a disturbed self. He would be restless with protest, defiance and anger within. He knew not on whom he bore so much grudge. Chhaya was warned. She had to avoid all such reasons for which Abhinna would be angry and displeased.

Within two or three days the excitement that the presence of the lady teacher had caused was over. Women of all age groups came not only to see her but to observe her minutely and to talk with her. They spoke to each other, "She seems good, neither proud nor showy and to be of cool temperament; affectionate and respectful. Do you remember the other lady teacher who was trying restlessly to anyhow leave the place? This village was not up to her choice. She always would boast of the things she had in her house and would point out the absence of those things in our village."

The school was at a distance of less than half a kilometer from Atanu's house. She would go to school walking through the village. After two lanes, there was a mango grove, and beyond the mango grove stood the school. While passing through the alleys, someone's coughing sound, the sound of someone's cleaning the throat, or the raucous guffaws of a group idling on a veranda or the recital of a few lines of some love songs would reach her ears. The small children's faces looked like gazing at some wonder. The housewives had the gesture of being delighted.

She would hear all such sounds and wicked suggestions while on the way to school with the two children. She understood the implications of all such things and would be delighted within. She would never be interested to know the source of such nuisance or about the man and his intention of doing that.

She would teach with great interest as if she was born for that work. She laughed with the children and loved them. She would encourage them to come up with answers to her questions. She would be annoyed at the absentminded and fickle students.

The Headmaster came every day but looked very dull as if he came to school against his will and was compelled to keep on chattering. He would give such an impression. The assistant teacher would seem to be in agony under the pressure of a lot of complaints and disturbances. Neither did anything good happen nor was there the possibility of anything good happening. No salary up to his requirement was paid to him. These boys would never do well in the examination, and so there was no meaning at all in putting so much labour.

This country would go to dogs due to the D.I and C.I offices. No one would do any work; if they did, it was after getting a bribe. Everywhere one noticed mismanagement, utter mismanagement!

He would threaten the children and adopt such techniques that the children would never come to him. He never cared for the Headmaster. He would warn- he who dared to do something against him would get a good dose. He would underestimate Chhaya and would sneer at her teaching style. Why did Chhaya perspire unnecessarily when nothing good happened anywhere in the country? He would ask this question indirectly knowing pretty well that there was no answer to it.

It was already half past eleven by the time dinner was over. The children had gone to bed much before. Atanu and Abhinna would dine together if the latter were at home. A different picture would come to Chhaya. At her house, Tushar, Pravir and her father would have their dinner together while domestic, and business matters crept in for discussion; at times giving scope for arguments and counter-arguments. Mother would always tell them that there ought to be silence at least at the time of taking food. Why did they make the dining table for the marketplace? No one would listen to her. Sometimes Chhaya would also take a side and give her opinion frankly.

Nothing like that happened there. Atanu and Abhinna would take their meals silently. Occasionally someone would ask to pass on the salt or the green chilli from the bowl. Salt and chilli came there without any sound. The water jug would be there near the pillar. Abhinna, while washing the mouth, would cleanse his throat and would startle the entire area with a raucous sound as if something stuck at the throat and pestered him, and he was overdone in trying to oust it.

The village would fall asleep before their dinner was over. No human voice would be heard at that time. All movements would remain held up for a night. Abhinna would go to the first room adjacent to the road and Atanu to the fourth room. The room which had been constructed for the saints and holy men was Chhaya's. The veranda was extended up to the front side of her room for which the terrace of the western parapet had to be cut. The room given to Chhaya was an extension of the original house.

The village road ran side by the side of the eastern parapet. The compound wall without plaster at a distance of fifteen to twenty feet was visible through the window at the western side of Chhaya's room. One could jump over it easily.

Chhaya and Atanu's wife would be the last to take their dinner. The veranda of Abhinna's room was connected to the kitchen. All the utensils used at night would be kept by the stairs near the kitchen. The domestic maid would sweep the courtyard and wash the utensils in the morning. The well was there near the kitchen.

Chhaya and Atanu's wife came back after locking the kitchen room. Atanu's daughter who was in class six was feeling weak due to a four-day-old fever. She would be raving a lot in a state of delirium and would grope for some way to get out of the bed in acute febrile condition. She did not sleep with Chhaya for the last five days. That day the son, who was in class four looked dull, he would also have a fever as he had all the symptoms of illness.

: "This seems to be a curse with this house." Atanu's disgusted wife said looking at the son lying on the bed. She had lost her patience with that problem. She said, "Once one is cured, the other would fall ill."

Touching the daughter's head, Chhaya said in a consoling tone, "No temperature! Perhaps the son has the same type of fever."

: "Exactly! She said being worried. Boasting of her farsightedness and wit, she said, "For that reason only I had told your brother to bring medicine for the son also as he would catch fever after his sister came round. Who would run to the hospital again, four Kilometres away? You see it yourself whether my prediction came true or not. The girl is still in bed and the son's turn has come already."

Chhaya would smile a little without giving any comment on that. She said such things were normal and they would happen. There was no justification in giving so much importance to such ordinary problems. Patting her vouja's back, she came out of the room.

The lantern in her room was burning dimly; she screwed up the wick a little and gave a glance all over. She had kept necessary books, notebooks, paper, pen, pencil etc. carefully. She would draw lines on the paper spread on the table to verify if the pen worked well. The matches were at hand. At the corner, there was a glass and a pitcher with water. The clothes hung from a rope. The other bed had been lying empty for the last four-five days due to the illness of Atanu's daughter. She used to sleep in madam's room.

The torch was at the pillow. After satisfying herself with its functioning, she would keep it with the wristwatch. In a niche on the wall, she had placed the idols and photos of gods. As usual, she prayed to them before going to bed. The lantern flame would dim and would extinguish at last. The odour of burnt kerosene would pervade the entire room. She would lie down on the bed.

Atanu's daughter would sleep with her mother as she had a fever. When she slept with Chhaya, she would see her and would take her to the right position in case her head slipped off the small pillow. Withdrawing her glance from her closed eyes, innocent face and the palm painted with *mehndi*, she would lie down.

That night, too, she lay down on bed. The extinguished lantern, as it were, had breathed its last through the odour of the burnt kerosene. She yawned. A strange sound had been there for the last four or five days which took possession of the entire room. That was the voice of seclusion, Chhaya said to herself. To just convince herself, she switched on the torch. It was not known what hour of the night it was. Although she had fallen asleep, her sub-conscious smelt of somebody's movement. Perhaps, that movement occurred not there but, in space, or on some unknown planet. It was very negligible and faint although, it was replete with ripples. And the ripples touched Chhaya's deep sleep slowly. Its slow and soft touch shook her slumber. Again, it would become still and stable the next moment.

It was just for a moment she felt that her flesh and bone along with her entire body would shrink centering on a point. She would withdraw herself to that point. Might be, such a feeling had been there in her without her knowledge, but the movement of more than one was perceived after that not on other planet or in space but in her own room. The subsequent perception was that the temporary and weak thing known as the sky could not hold itself. Chhaya could not prevent a terrible horror. The sky fell down in a thousand fragments. Chhaya could never tell if the tiles of the roof fell down also or were about to fall.

An inhuman power pervaded right from the earth to the horizon. That power had been stubborn and invincible; it was keen and determined too. Although it was beyond identification due to darkness; it, like a steel chest, had overpowered her by tremendous pressure. Her struggling hands lay motionless owing to an unseen heaviness. The material stuffed in her mouth had choked her cries and screams. Before she lost her consciousness and became inoperative, she felt that all her clothes were being taken off and her protest was going in vain. And within a benumbed inertness, she had been almost dead.

Atanu was not aware of how his sleep was disrupted.

It was not only that his sleep got interrupted,but a terrible shock lifted him from the bed. He could not know instantly why he became panicky in his own house. His troubled heart palpitated restlessly. An involuntary loud voice— "Who?" came out.

There was no answer to this query. Atanu could hear it distinctly that there was not one, a group ran westward in frantic haste. His entire body horripilated. He gave a loud cry, "Who's there?"

Everything was mute and still. As if, 'who's there' as a question was not worthy enough for getting an answer. So, for this reason, a cold wave spread from the toe to the tip. He felt it necessary to come out for ascertaining what would be his next step.

Then there was the fear and the apprehension of some devastation somewhere. Flabbergasted, he only gave out a loud scream. The door of his room was shut from outside. Mysterious! Dangerous and enigmatic too!

He battered the door. He so battered and banged it as if the setting of the door by man were an unpardonable blunder. Never had he thought of taking the door for a vexing hurdle and fighting against it. Who kept him confined in his room and for what reason he did so? Perplexed and impatient like a cat on hot bricks he banged the door and cried for help.

The shrieking and banging got scattered on the silent and speechless state of the night and its darkness. It turned back to him taking the shape of an echo. Was it an echo really? After a few moments, he rectified the mistake. Abhinna too was banging the door of his room. The same banging! The same cry! All of the family had been confined in their rooms. The sick son's cry got fused with the eager and earnest appeal of the wife to open the door. Never had the house been so separated from the earth. Everything appeared dreadful and fatal in the vicious clutch of some unknown and invincible power.

At first, Abhinna's door broke with a sound disregarding the sound of a terrible thunder. The light of his torch pierced the darkness that had captured them so long. He opened the doors of other two rooms that had been shut from outside.

Atanu and his children stood perplexed on the veranda in a state of flux due to the horror. They looked anemic and stupid.

: "How is that?"

: "Some men had come."

: "Definitely; otherwise how could doors be shut from outside?"

: "Nothing is clear."

: "Not one, there were more than one."

: "But they..."

: "I've heard them running away."

Not only that; they told many more things in panting whispers, and that too, all of them together. The terror came, imprisoned them and ran away. They could not know what devastations it had wrought before it vanished.

H e y, h e y Chhaya, Chhaya-

Chhaya's name was still reverberating in the void of darkness. And all were animated. That time their foot and brain were spirited and lively, not stagnant. All their torches focussed at Chhaya's room.

And here was the horrible difference. Here, the door was not shut from outside. It remained connected with the outside void and gloom. To allow free and easy passage to and fro the room, the two door panels hung from their wooden frame.

And there was the horrible sight. Had the torch known how to revolt, it would have cried, "I defy the command of the torch button. My light will never fall on the scene like this."

Their eyes got closed for they had the liberty to hide behind the lids.

All their intellectual faculties were crushed. They, at that terrible moment, could not know if their legs and hands had slipped off their bodies.

It was Atanu's wife who regained her consciousness first. She covered Chhaya's bare body with someone's abandoned cloth that had stuck between the bed and the floor. But it was not that easy to remove the stubborn lump of material from her mouth. Atanu freed both her hands tied with the leg of the bed.

Unexpected, horrendous and heart rending! Much more than this was the horrible significance of that very scene which sneered at their knowledge and experience. It overwhelmed them, made them stupid and handicapped. They had no measure to encounter that. Even they had no way out to hold the present state of awful affairs.

They had been shaken by the sudden and tremendous invasion. Never-seen-before grief and pity thoroughly dishevelled them. Fury and resentment got no platform, as none had been there yet to express themselves. The target of anger and resentment was the unknown malefactor; even the Creator Himself whose creation contained devastative evil.

Atanu's wife was about to ask what all that had been and how it happened but failed to articulate. She covered her face with her palms; withdrew her look and wept like a destitute orphan standing helplessly at a corner of the room. Till then Atanu's tears had been looking for an outlet. His tears wanted to overflow, not through the eyes alone but through all the pores of hair of his entire body. He tried to hold himself.

But Abhinna came out, and standing in the courtyard he threw challenges at the top of his voice, "Show yourself if at all you have any manliness, come, fight with me, defeat me if you could, cut me into pieces. That would be your chivalry. Come. Come out from the niche you are hiding. Go and ask your mothers... you damn cowards, fie on you. Hideously under the cover of darkness...fie, fie on you!"

To know what shape takes language out of a mixture of anger and anguish one should hear that futile cry of Abhinna. The village slept under silence, trees were dumb, and the sky was indifferent. Penetrated into these were Abhinna's anger and anguish.

Not known who lighted the lantern. In that scarce and smoky light, Chhaya did not appear like any human being on this planet. Her identity had been changed. She seemed a stranger that no one had seen before. There was the fall of that affectionate, passionate and humble soul who after dinner had infused courage in her *vouja* and had lovingly caressed the sleeping children.

Who was that disordered, wounded and ravished human being who for the last few days had been intimately connected with the family? Her dishevelled hairs were searching for their own place. There were injury marks on the face, on the hands, and on the entire body; torn and displaced were all her clothing. No one could imagine what bestial power could work out such heartless and horrible havoc and for how long it continued.

The two ailing children looked shocked and petrified. They could not comprehend anything but were in a sobbing state after seeing Chhaya's condition. They had not joined with their mother as the reason for their mother's weeping was known to them. They only understood that something had happened to madam.

It was Atanu who became conscious of the children's presence there. He took them out of the room. His wife, at her wit's end, wanted only to lift Chhaya onto her breast and to caress the wounds on her body. She wished she made up her dishevelled hairs.

Extending her hands at her, she showed her unbound sympathy in a choking voice, "How it happened, Chhaya! Ever I was cursed with these eyes to see it! And it had to happen in my house?"

For the first time, there was some movement in her body. She licked her lips and became conscious that there was nothing aqueous in her body. In a feeble voice, she uttered, "Vouja, a little water!"

Vouja was taken aback while filling the glass with water. How was it after such an incident Chhaya's voice had been unperturbed and unemotional? Why was she not crying? There would be little relief if she cried!

Vouja took back the glass and extended her hand to bring her clothes in order. Chhaya forbade her in the same heavy tone- "Don't touch me, vouja, this body has been polluted. Besides, I have to go to the Police Station. How would you know the cloth and the bed to have been drenched in blood?"

Chhaya had a glass of hot milk after half an hour. There was unbearable pain all over the body. She tried to get up. She said to herself, "No pain could check me. Why, what for the body has preserved the thing called pain after losing everything?"

By the morning she could finish her daily chores except for the bath. She had a faint idea that she had to go to the Police Station and to the hospital from there. After that only she would think about what was and what was not necessary for her body.

: "Madam, should I go to your house? "Atanu was more polite and sympathetic.

Chhaya looked at him. No reaction on her swollen face was visible. She seemed undecided. She said, "What for?"

Atanu was astounded. What answer would he give to that question? He said, "They should know about such a serious thing. Your brothers might come to some help." Atanu argued.

; "Can you not do that what my brothers would do?" Chhaya asked without taking any time.

Perplexed, all of them melted. Never in their lifetime had Atanu or Abhinna heard such an immaculate and unpretentious sentence. The intimate touch in it delighted them. But, Abhinna who stood there proposed, "No, not you, I'll go with the ma'am to the Police Station or to the hospital, whatsoever, I'll be there with her."

It was daybreak. By this time Chhaya would get up. With a smile, vouja would ask, "Will you like a tea?" As a routine, everyday she would be busy supervising the children's homework and correcting the copies. Then she would take her bath followed by breakfast and get ready for the school.

The entire village had been shaken by nine that morning. The boughs of the trees hung down out of shame and guilt consciousness. The cattle too could not raise their heads. The village road lay unconscious. Fragments of agony scattered from the beaks of the birds. The villagers would start gathering on the veranda, in the courtyard, and on the road in front of Atanu's house.

Tears rolled down from the eyes of women when Chhaya came out of her room to go up to Abhinna ready with the motorcycle. Alas! The poor girl was not able to walk.

She would not take vouja's help also. How ugly her figure looked! They were churned within to see her outraged body in torn clothes. This rape was not with Chhaya or Atanu's house; it was a sexual assault on the entire village. Everyone was alarmed at the horrible and ugly picture of hell wrought by rape.

Chhaya was not in a position of looking at anyone. Everyone there stood petrified to see her not crying. There was no place for any emotion on her defiled face. She appeared solemn; possibly unperturbed. This was enough to arouse restlessness in the souls of many. Were the nerves that looked so soft and delicate made of steel?

Chhaya had to struggle a lot to get on to the pillion seat of the motorbike. The picture of agony reflected on her face at the time she tried to get on the bike. Was there any stamina and determination still left in her despite the severe pain to sit on the bike?

She gave an indifferent look at the gathering over there. There was no language, no message in that look. Only a suggestion like "I am going, I have to go not known how far" was there. She had not expressed any gratitude to the people for sympathizing with her. She had no need for it. She had not also expressed any annoyance as to why they gathered there leaving their work. To her utter surprise, no suggestion of anger, hatred and determination for taking revenge was there.

After parking the motorcycle, Abhinna waited until Chhaya climbed up the stairs of the Police Station. All alert, he was with Chhaya. The Officer-in-charge had already come. Before she said something, he said, "Please be seated in that chair, Madam."

The officer's gaze concentrated on Chhaya's face. His experience prompted that there had been sure and severe deviation of law and humanitarianism. By the time he withdrew his look from Abhinna, Chhaya's extended hand had held before him a piece of paper. The unperturbed and grave tone pronounced the single word-FIR.

The Officer was going through it, giving intermittent looks at Chhaya. It took time to finish reading the contents of two pages. He put it on the table under the care of a paperweight. Leaning back in the chair, he observed Chhaya in silence. A deep sigh! Was it because of a new problem or thinking about the fall of man; or was it a gesture of sympathy to Chhaya? Nothing could be ascertained.

He was going to lift the paperweight but withheld. Was there anguish and sympathy in his voice? Not sure. But his first reaction was, "I am sorry, such a thing happened, very bad, damn bad!

: "We want the immediate arrest of the miscreants. We, all the people of our village have been utterly lost in grief for this. Believe me, they are crying." Abhinna had been bit excited towards the end.

The officer did not even look at him as if an unimportant, ludicrous thing was being represented.

: It took place inside the room; how many were there?" He asked.

: "I could not know, as I had lost my consciousness." She said. Her voice was firm and distinct.

: "Were they drunk? The officer asked.

He added further, "Well, you can't talk about all as

you had no sense but in what condition were the first one or two? Were they drunk?"

: Yes. Said Chhaya.

: "Whom do you suspect? Did you have any rift with anyone or animosity or anything like the sort with anyone?"

: I can't suspect anyone, I had no hostility, no conflict and even no argument with anyone." Chhaya gave her statements as before in a calm and bold voice. Dissatisfaction spread over the officer's face. He was going to find out something out of the FIR. He said, "It may be presumed that this is the work of some guys of the village. You have mentioned that you had shut the door from within. You had not opened that. Then how did the rascals get into the room? How did they come?" His question approximated a threat.

Chhaya could not give any answer to that question. But she did not look disturbed, confounded or pathetic. She did not also shrink for not being able to provide information essential for solving the mystery. She said, "That is incomprehensible for me too. I don't know."

: "Do you keep the room under lock always; I mean when you are out?" The officer enquired.

: "I don't think it necessary," Chhaya said. "I stay with an established and respectable family of the village. In case I went to other rooms, I would only bolt it from outside. I don't lock the room always."

The officer thumped mildly on the table. He said as if discovering something, "We have to go to the spot for enquiry. It is likely that someone might have been there beforehand without your knowledge, but I am not sure. We will have to take you to the hospital, have you come prepared for that?" Bitter disgust was clearly writ on his face.

: "Yes," was Chhaya's brief reply.

Then he started to write something. Chhaya's FIR was registered perhaps. The pen he was writing with was not functioning well. A drop of ink fell on the paper. Even at that time, Chhaya was delighted a little having seen the fury and helplessness of the officer. The drop of ink on the paper sneered and challenged him, and waited to see how the officer would face it.

The officer gave a retreat and took the help of the *Havildar*. The *havildar* took a piece of cloth out of the drawer, the original colour of which had been lost under the random plaster of black ink. The pen for time and again would create this problem and the piece of cloth was in service to solve the problem. The register got disfigured, but that drop of ink didn't like to go into the cloth. It spread over the page.

: "What did you do, you useless?" The officer's mood was off; he shouted, "Can't you bring a drop of ink to your control?" Without saying anything the havildar left the place undisturbed. He gave an impression that still bitterer rebuke would have no impact on him.

Further, what a great thing happened if a small space of the page was smeared with ink? Sorts of ink like this are everywhere! Countless things get disfigured and become ugly. Eventuality is there always and everywhere.

Fatigue, terrible inflammation and pain aggravated slowly. The entire body ached due to the fresh wounds. At times, she thought that it was beyond her tolerance. Sitting, standing and walking would not be possible; neither at present nor in future. The faith that the agony would have an end was losing ground gradually. Chhaya saw Abhinna stand leaning against a wall. He was prepared to help her in every way. The officer wrote and read it. It was not up to his mark. He would strike it and would think seriously and would write again despite the non-cooperation of the pen.

: "Would you repent in future for having brought the matter to the police?" asked the officer.

Chhaya could not understand the question correctly; she contracted her eyebrows and begged his pardon.

: "What I mean to say is..."He leaned against the chair again. Apprehending his words might irritate or discourage her, he smiled a little so that his words would not have any jagged or jarring impact on her. He said, "Generally, people suppress such incidents so that the society would not know the victim. You are young. Your future might be stained if the matter is made public. You, at your personal level, might not be benefited in any way if the culprits were taken to task. On the contrary, the rascals might be revengeful thinking of the possibility of being apprehended and so; they might do some further harm to you. Have you pondered over these aspects?"

The officer paused here for some time and tried to read the reaction on her face. There was no sign of any impact. Chhaya kept on listening to him mindfully as before with the same objective detachment and seriousness. She did not say anything as she knew that the officer had not completed.

Actually, it was not complete. He resumed, "I hope you have kept all these in view and have taken the step judiciously. Please don't mind if I say that this is an audacious step, may be dangerous also. That would be like suicide if you repented for having taken this step."

: "You said all these as my well-wisher, didn't you? Chhaya gave a straight look at the officer.

: "Yes, absolutely!" He said emphatically. Further, he

said, "I am sorry, in fact, at a loss to see your miserable condition. I am not sure if you have done a wise thing in giving the FIR and how your family, your relatives, and the society will take this step of yours."

He could not conclude in the right way. He shook his head and indicated that the problem would not end by giving the FIR; rather it would start and might go beyond control.

: "Certainly you are not saying that the victim would bear with the rape and would not give any FIR. Family, society and relatives- nobody would stand in support if she complained. The future would be marred, and there would be the apprehension of revenge also. Do you say this exactly? Do you say like this as an officer or, excuse me, you would say like this also as the victim's father or brother?" Her version could be of much impact for she gave it in calm and normal voice without being least excited.

The officer shrank as he felt offended. Readily he had no words. He admitted to himself that his calculations had gone wrong. He could not assess her power and determination. "Maybe, someone might have instigated such an innocent, stupid and pathetic looking victim to lodge the complaint at the Police Station. She had no understanding that such a complaint might have serious repercussions on her and on her family. She hadn't the right knowledge of it. Someone instigated her, and sticking to an erroneous and momentary pig-headedness she came here." He had thought like this.

Although the officer did not like it, he corrected his assessment of Chhaya. Chhaya's words hurt his sentiments very much. It was not acceptable to him as he never expected to meet a person disagreeable to him, that too in his Police Station.

: "And about digesting it for fear of humiliation and suppressing the matter, why should I be afraid of anybody and be ashamed?" There was no change in her voice. She continued, "I in this condition and in this dress can make a round of any city, the whole world even. I can give a frank and free description of the last night's episode. I want the arrest of the culprits. Let a message reach them that their heinous crime can never be excused. For fear of their revenge, a victim should never live in a state of utter helplessness and die a daily death. I have come here not to express shame for my misfortune but to protest against that."

She was neither panting nor excited. What to speak of the fire usually belched out during a lecture on such topic, there was not the slightest warmth in her voice. She had not completed what she wanted to say: "I have not thought of reforming the society through this nor have I thought of taking revenge on the miscreants. Let the culprits be identified. That is my target. Who would have I approached for this purpose? Your actions will impose control over crimes and criminals."

Chhaya sat with the visible wounds and with the invisible and inexpressible pain and anguish. But she seemed to be very vast and higher than the wounds. Strangely, she looked pure and clean. The culprits would look pitiably ordinary if they stood by her. The officer marked another thing. Chhaya's thought was neither weak nor disorganized. He had no confidence as to convince or misguide her. All these added importance and prestige to Chhaya's personality.

But the way Chhaya asserted herself was not liked by the officer. She sought the help of the police but would not pray for it. She had no humility. She would have read that it was the duty of the police to find out the antisocial elements. Their service was meant for that. That is true of course, but for that, a lot of things including flattery needed to be done.

Perhaps, this lady who was fresh in the teaching profession was yet to learn this. Nothing happens precisely as per the theories. The officer had no fascination to love Chhaya's personality, to be enchanted by her words or to take prompt action on getting her complaint; on the contrary, he could not digest the way Chhaya proved him inferior in conversation and arguments. His ego had been seriously hurt.

Chhaya was in the police jeep half an hour after this. Hospital. The lady doctor was surrounded by many people. Chhaya and Abhinna were on a bench. Abhinna wanted to assist her, to do something to lessen her pain-some water, tea or tiffin. She had a glass of water in a restaurant after returning from the Police Station. She wasn't interested to eat or at least to have a cup of tea.

She was in a fix. Should she go to Mohangarh or to her room with Abhinna after the hospital formalities were over? However, it would not be possible to go to school the next day. First, she had to recover. For that, she had no other way out except going to her parents. She was afraid that there would be an untoward situation at home when they heard of her plight. Her mother would break her head on the wall. How would father raise his head high in the street? How would brother Tushar and Pravir face the people in the market?

The police personnel escorting her informed the Lady Doctor that the rape victim needed immediate medical attention as her condition was very grave. She would take rest as soon as the report of the medical examination had been prepared.

: "Call her in." The doctor said and waited in the curtained chamber. A look at Chhaya shook her with fear and compassion. Her mouth lost the power of speech for some moments.

What was there to see, what was there to examine!

She, her entire body and face bore the evidence of rape. No person with sense could ever make anyone so ugly. It appeared as if a hundred monsters had come out with tooth and claw to work out such ruin. Possibly, because she was a woman, her inner being shook out of empathy and revolt.

How she desired to caress the wounds on Chhaya's body! Oh, had there been such medicament with her, at the simple touch of which the terrible cracks and ruptures on her body would have vanished!

: "There must have been severe bleeding," the doctor said. Her voice was soaked with sympathy and emotion.

: "Yes, excessive. Madam, I was afraid that all my blood would drain out. Perhaps it has." She said.

Very astonishingly Chhaya was speaking normally in a calm voice. There was no sentimentality either. The doctor became more attentive in examining her as she had the curiosity to know what elements she was made of.

: "There must be spasm and pain." She said and wanted an answer.

: "It was beyond my imagination that a body could bear such pain and agony. What to speak of walking, it's difficult to raise the hand even." Chhaya said.

Withdrawing her look from Chhaya, she started filling up a form.

: "Ma'am, will I be alright soon?" Now only she seemed eager.

: "The injury is not ordinary." Busy in writing, she

looked at her for a moment and said, "Here I prescribe some medicines along with an injection. It will take some time for you to come round. You are in a hurry. I understand. That is natural."

: "I want to go back to the classroom as soon as possible." The doctor's sympathy had made her frank. She said involuntarily, "Ma'am, no other place will be suitable for me. I don't believe others will readily accept me."

: "I understand." Having said this, she handed over the paper advising her complete rest. She fixed her gaze on Chhaya's face for a while and said, "It is a good thing that you have not broken down. Stay bold and unyielding; never give in to anyone or anything. Your softness would encourage others to fall on you. If you feel necessary, you are welcome always to see me. All my deep love and good wishes are and will be there for you forever."

Chhaya's inner being was shaken by these words. Her lips quivered involuntarily. Her brows contracted. As it were, she was about to decant herself, but she held herself. She touched the doctor's feet and came out.

There was a fortuitous scene near the hospital portico. Abhinna was not alone there. A small gathering was already there comprising two teachers and the peon of her school, teachers of other schools and about thirty villagers. Seeing them, Chhaya realized with what sincerity they had arrived there. How profoundly intimate and pure their feeling was for her! The anxiety-ridden faces of the people there spoke of their helplessness. Despite all eagerness, they would have no share of Chhaya's pain and agony; yet their insides were filled with despair arising out of their utter helplessness. At the time of coming to the Police Station some villagers cried literally; and now while returning, there was a rendezvous of caring looks.

There was such a wave that fortified Chhaya's courage enhancing her self-confidence. She would face the world.

Chhaya folded her hands to salute the crowd as a mark of respect. The tiny smile on her face was able to outdo the shattering pangs of her aching body. She didn't complain; instead, she expressed her gratitude by way of asking the Head Master, "Sir, you all are here, there's none in the school then!"

The Head Master could not say anything. His face tried to seize unbound cordiality and compassion. He withdrew his face from her to wipe the tear with his dhoti's pleats. A young teacher said on behalf of the Head Master and all the teachers, "What would we do in the school? How could we teach the students after hearing about the barbaric incident! Of course, we will be back in the class. We will wait for eight to ten days. If by that time the rascals are not arrested all schools will remain closed. We will go on the rally, hunger strike and will *gherao* the Police Station. We will paralyze the offices from the D.I's to D.P.I's. No minister, no secretary can come out. Beginning from the DG to the Officer-in-Charge, all will be confined to their houses only. Madam, this ravishment is not on you alone, it is the ravishment of all educational institutions and of all lady teachers."

All of them fell thunderstruck. If the blood was inflamed, the bones would be restless to crush the stone, concrete and even, steel. And, if the resolutions were transformed to action to wipe out crimes, this speech spirited with excitement would be enough to destroy inactivity and indifference like magic. Then, in that case, the life lying dormant within would become restless to be functional.

All stood spellbound and focussed their attention on the young teacher who tried to establish himself as a teacher-leader. The natural hubbub of the hospital had come to a standstill. The busy movement of the patients and their attendants, the doctor and his stethoscope, the nurse and the tray she carried, and the sweeper and his broomstick- all froze into a still and silent picture.

Chhaya became conscious when the young teacher came near her and said, "The entire teaching community is with you. My regards and good wishes to you! You came to the Police Station, lodged the FIR. It's not a small thing. This is a moral victory." And then lowering his tone he expressed helplessness: "It's true, we can't repair the damage done to you nor can we take out the pain and agony from you. If it were possible, trust me please, only I would have taken all your agonies."

Disfigured Chhaya shrivelled further in humility. She would go, and the police would also go with her for spot inquiry. Chhaya had no words; she folded her hands again to express her gratitude. Her face gave the indication that she was totally overwhelmed by their response.

It was three o'clock by the time they reached Atanu's house. Abhinna was sure that Chhaya could walk. Hence, his help was not that necessary. He had not known the two brothers of Chhaya- Tushar and Pravir? They had reached there after being informed by someone. Chhaya saw them. She was not at all relieved or happy. How would she encounter their presence there? There was no way. Their presence created sad vibrations of pity in her.

Chhaya looked away from them after a moment as if the two were strangers to her. She had to struggle to enter the room. These two under a terrible trauma had been confounded and in a state of flux to see Chhaya. Was she their sister? Was that their Chhaya, the deformed one, bearing the heavy weight of the blows and the throes? They had no idea why mangled Chhaya looked distant and magnified. Both of them seemed comparatively small and insignificant.

: "Don't tell her anything now." Tushar advised Pravir. They were still standing on the road unconnected and unrelated.

: "Better we took her home. "Pravir said in a choked voice; in fact, he wiped his eyes. "Oh, it's unbearable, my heart shatters into pieces. Both father and mother will die to see her; they can't stand the sight. Oh, What a misfortune!" Pravir was almost lost.

Tushar did not give him any consolation as he would try to hold himself from breaking down. The crowd of the village people was thickening, and Tushar and Pravir were getting impatient. It had not been known to anyone when the police would reach the spot of the crime.

Atanu came hastily on to the road. He had known Pravir. He took it to himself and was prepared to accept any punishment. The hellish havoc took place in his house when he was very much present at home. Atanu, not in a position of excusing himself held Pravir's hands and said, "Kill me; I have no right to live any further. I don't care what would happen to my family. Come, someone cut me into pieces. That would be my true penance and there only would be my deliverance."

This drama would have continued further on the road, had the police jeep not reached then. The Officer-in-charge along with two others examined the room and its surrounding. There continued the interrogation, "Did

Chhaya sleep there in the last room, alone? When was the dinner over? Does she remember if she had bolted the room from outside and if it had been unbolted at the time she entered the room after dinner?" The officer recorded all the statements.

The rascals had left no clues. It seemed to be the work of the village youths. They had been quite acquainted with that room. Since Atanu's daughter had a fever, she had not been sleeping with Chhaya for the last three-four nights. Chhaya would not bolt the door from outside always. The rogues had marked that. But, the most irresponsible thing was to keep her in the last room. Chhaya didn't remember if the room had been bolted from without while coming into the room after dinner. Anyway, it's pre-planned and neatly designed. How dare they; bolting all doors from outside...!

He shook his head and tried to wipe the hellish event off his head.

: "Sir, how soon do you think the beasts can be chained?" Abhinna asked.

The officer looked at him and didn't hide his disgust. First, he thought that the question was not worth answering but however, having a glass of sorbet he said, "How can I say? Can anyone say? We will try to find them out to cut them into size." He passed on the empty glass and wiped his face with his hanky. Everyone was pessimistic about it. It was not known why there wasn't any life in his voice.

x x x x

The bikes of the two halted together in front of the house that lay senseless, speechless and motionless like a carcass. Father sat in the passage-room and

Mother on the kitchen veranda with hands on her head. Sitting there, she would wipe the tears from time to time. Chhaya's sister-in-law stood leaning against a pillar after lighting the evening-wick before the *tulsi.* The flame flickered. It extinguished, a slim line of smoke ascended like the last breath. In no time it got lost in the air. A hundred watt bulb burnt hesitatingly. A cold and pathetic atmosphere!

While walking before Gananath, it seemed to Chhaya as if her knee would loosen and slip off and the spine would split into thousand pieces. Father saw Chhaya walking and withdrew his glance from her out of utter anguish. Had he taught her to walk like that? She had not even looked so hopeless and undone when she tottered with her immature and unstable steps. Standing before her at a distance and extending his hand he had beckoned her 'come dear come'. Was that really the babyhood of this present Chhaya? What type of misfortune was that! Beckoning 'come dear come' and extending the hands had become the part of old history. No further could he sit there, he climbed up the stairs to the terrace.

The silent grief of Gananath took the shape of heart rending wailing in her mother. "My dear; my jewel! Why didn't I die? Were you fated for this?" She was not able to say anything more. She caressed Chhaya's entire body. Every bit of her was harassed. The newly built building seemed to shake.

Chhaya did not make any effort to free herself from the ring of her embrace, her wailing and her tears. She stood and waited for the time when her mother would be a little relieved of the grief. She would be relieved for the grief would never be permanent.

: "Stop now." Her mother could not believe that the

calm and unperturbed voice was of Chhaya's. Dumbfounded she looked at Chhaya in tearful eyes. She had not been conscious that she had stopped crying.

: "What is the use of crying like this? " Chhaya asked as if she didn't approve of a thing like crying.

: "What did you say, what use?" The mother protested. This time she was sentimental. "I won't cry; I will be at ease after what has happened to you. Look- she asks me why I am crying. She says there's no need of it." She was going to continue her sobbing.

: "Stop, I say." This time it approximated a threat. This was Chhaya's first loud advice after the incident. She said again, "Nothing has happened to me. Stop crying." Then Chhaya was in her room.

No one in the family could believe how such a heart rending episode full of events became eventless. The victim presented herself as one unaffected. She protested when others broke their heads for that. She would look undisturbed despite her terribly broken frame. She declared that nothing had happened to her. What could be told of her; was there any befitting adjective for her?

But that was not exactly the reality. Chhaya was alone in a room. On switching off the light, she felt to be no more within a safe zone. The walls collapsed; from under the floor, from the horizon and from the sky came out the claws and the teeth. Her mouth was gagged, and her hands were tied. A determined bestial force was tearing her. She would not be in bed, not in the room, not in her known world; she would not be anywhere. She could not know where she was; she was getting lost into nothingness.

Had she been lost; had she been finished, she would have been liberated. She wouldn't have been there to have a feel of herself. There was so much pain and agony to bear yet, her body would not remain her previous body even after returning to her room and to her bed. What an irony! Despite the ravishment, the body would be hers!

Her eyelids would drop. And they would open again in apprehension and hallucination. The mouth would be dry and the body wet with perspiration.

She switched on the light. Was there anyone under the bed or in any secret place- in the wind or in the pooja room? How strong were the grille and panel of the window! Would it open under the pressure of someone's hand without making any sound? And the misfortune would befall at the moment when she in her drowsy state would cry, "who, who." She went out and drank some water. Then she fell asleep in the early hours of the morning till 9.

By 10 in the morning, she had finished her morning chores. She heard her father say in the passage hall, "Why would you disturb her? She is not in good condition. She is not in a position to meet anyone."

: "Who?" Chhaya was already there.

A young man was there. "I am Amiya," he introduced himself. "I work for a Newspaper. I came to have an interview with you."

That time he wanted the permission from her, not from Gananath. Chhaya said," Father thought I was taking rest." Then she in the way of seeking her father's permission said, "Father, let me talk with the gentleman for some time." Thereby she gave an indirect hint that it would be better if he were not there.

: "I reached there when you were leaving the Police Station." Amiya said this after they took their seats. He resumed, "I had no difficulty in getting the copy of your FIR and the case number. You had to return home via the hospital. It had also been fixed that the police were to go to the spot."

Amiya paused and said withdrawing his glance from Chhaya who was listening to him with rapt attention, "I have seen how you walked yesterday. The agony was getting automatically written on your face despite your efforts to suppress it. This condition of yours held me back from disturbing you. Now also you have pain. I know it; still, I want to make a story about you for our Weekly. I have already talked to the Editor. He has also given me an encouraging nod for that."

Chhaya did not think of anything to be said after that. She only looked at Amiya intently. Amiya said, "Such things do take place every now and then, but for various reasons, the matter doesn't reach the police. That's why we want to present your case in our Weekly. That would create the awareness. Further, it will exert pressure on the police to be prompt."

Having completed, he was about to lean against the chair; but it occurred to him that he had forgotten to tell an important thing. He said, "I, on my behalf and on behalf of our Newspaper congratulate you and appreciate your uncommon courage. You will have our full support for this. You are going to set an example. This incident has a great social and humanitarian relevance."

There was silence. Chhaya could not think of where to start her story. Amiya had not only been astonished; he had been slightly hurt also to see that his words could not arouse the least interest in her. What to speak of her being delighted and overwhelmed by his talk, there was a smile on her lips instead indicating that she had no need for all that. Amiya was discouraged.

: "I am an example and model for others!" Her smile

beamed further. With all politeness, she said, "What all these are you talking of? My courage would create awareness. Perhaps people will know and praise me. I haven't thought of all these.

Looking away from Amiya, she said in a heavy tone, "I don't want such big things. Believe me, I haven't thought from that perspective at all, there is no need for it."

She said in her natural tone, "One thing has become clear for me. Power causing great havoc is here, there and everywhere. Simply a slight crack due to carelessness or absent-mindedness is enough for it to creep in. It enters to create havoc when a man is alone, pitiably alone and helpless. Father, mother, brother or well-wisher — none can be of much use then."

She smiled in the way of begging pardon and continued, "No Amiya babu is there to speak a word of sympathy to me; neither his newspaper nor his weekly!

Yesterday, a well-wisher fellow teacher had been quite enthusiastic about giving a fight for me. To be a part of my struggle, he declared to deadlock the entire administration if necessary. Why should I be skeptic about him or his way of looking at things? That was natural and spontaneous. But I know it is a temporal whim. It will have its web in a day or two. This tidal wave would weaken and get lost. I don't blame anyone. This is the truth. The visage of reality is disappointing!

No one had ever impressed Amiya like Chhaya. So pure and unaffected was her thought! It had delighted him very much without his knowledge. There were four to five marks of injury on her face, all swollen and blackened. The lower lip was cracked and deformed; similar signs were there on the neck. The wounds on the wrists were still looking fresh. Amiya got back to himself. Why and how such a person, ruined out and out, would be exulted in delight and take this world for a safe place?

He gave a brief smile and said, "You have become a cynic. Anyone in your place would be like this."

Chhaya looked moron. She said politely, "I could not get at that word."

: "Cynic; he tried to explain its meaning, "It means one with no faith in human virtues or human relations. A cynic is generally pessimistic by disposition." His smile broadened. He said, "Such a person only finds fault with others and pours scorn on them. No; I don't say it at all that your thought has reached such a stage."

Perhaps, during their entire conversation Chhaya, for the first time laughed so open-heartedly. She said, "You took me to be like this? I was only telling about the havoc-causing power and man's loneliness. I was telling about the brief existence of his interest and enthusiasm. I exist even after the havoc. I would carry on my efforts to live well. I love life. I don't know if a cynic thinks like this."

Chhaya's face looked dreamy. Possibly, it was a plan for the future; a preparation to have the taste of life. This appealed to Amiya the most.

: "Then what do you say?" Do you consent to our flashing your story in our Weekly?" asked Amiya.

: "Do you think it necessary?" Pensive Chhaya asked a little while after.

: "Yes," said Amiya emphatically. "Of course, it's a different thing if you have any objection to it." He added.

That was Amiya's bid for Chhaya to decide. She, in fact, dwindled a little. She said, "Your story will drag me into an issue. I am not doing all these to be in the news. I did what was necessary. If need be, I will proceed further in this direction. It didn't matter if there were discussions on it on the pages of newspapers or not,"she said.

She remained silent for some time. Amiya waited for her. He knew that Chhaya had not finished.

Raising her head, she said, "If my case was published in your Weekly, the issue would have a greater focus, wouldn't it? Some readers would get strange excitement from that. Why some, many would crave for that thinking-wow! The molesters managed to escape after doing that! Till now the police are without any clue. If we could do that! Wouldn't many of them who do not know about the incident correctly take me for a cheap woman? They may have the idea that my behaviour might have provoked the rascals. They might have got some indications from me."

Chhaya was very frank and forthright. What boldness and confidence she exuded! There was a vibration in Amiya; it touched his heart for it was impregnated with much insight and wisdom. Chhaya's assessment of human nature was so flawless.

He was going to praise her, but Chhaya's words interrupted him. This time her voice was depressed and cheerless. "Am I cheap and easy? Whom and how will I convince that I am not at all like that? What sort of provoking hints did they get from me? How did that hint look like? That is the mystery for me. Even the strictest introspection doesn't give me any clues."

Amiya melted at this point. He was astounded as she told all these in her normal voice although two drops of tear rolled down her face. A drop of tear stopped on the cheek, and the other rolled further down onto the swollen lip.

Amiya sat there as before. He waited for that moment when Chhaya would wipe the tears. She did it with the corner of her saree and smiled like pitying her own self as if she had fallen on to the earth. Straightening herself, she said, "Excuse me; I didn't feel like crying since the incident. The tears rolled down before you; I had no control over them."

It was beyond expectation that Amiya would get so much experience and wisdom, and knowledge about human life from Chhaya in so brief a time. He would have told something about cheap and easy innuendos but did not. Chhaya's mental state was not in a favourable condition to receive that. A molester never identifies if a woman was really cheap or easy. Why should he wait for the woman to propose welcoming his bestiality? He needs the flesh. All his desire, design and execution concentrate on the body, its flesh.

: "Wouldn't you like a tea? You have been talking since long. This kind gesture of yours will keep me obliged. Need I tell this?" Chhaya was getting back to normalcy.

Amiya was elated again. No one had requested him in such a manner. He said, "I would like a glass of water, instead; I was about to ask for it."

Amiya sat in a street tea shop. Chhaya's conduct and the conversation had a tremendous impact on him. He had been associated with an established Newspaper of the Capital after being jobless for some days after his P.G. He stayed at the Capital. He had gone to the Police Station to help a relative during his stay at his native place, Chandanpur. There he knew about the Chhaya issue.

The interest to make a story on her alone had brought him to Chhaya's house.

It was not possible to place the story in the Weekly. This cannot be taken as Chhaya's non-cooperation. Her disinterest in this matter dissuaded him from that. But he was not disappointed; rather, he was happy to have met Chhaya. His motorcycle was in the Capital. He had been to his village by bus. He borrowed a bicycle from someone to meet Chhaya. He had to cover a long distance. The labour was not meaningless, however. It is not that he would only remember Chhaya; he would love, nay respect her perhaps. She was an exception, a rare lady. So much of maturity at such a young age and with such education! So beautiful and loving a personality with crystal clear thought and consideration! He was highly impressed.

He had finished the tea unmindfully. It was almost noon. The weather was partly sunny and partly clouded. The clouds of different patterns held a competition in light and shade. The tea was not bad. That was the reason that attracted the tea addicts to that shop. There was a natural atmosphere of joking, laughing and merrymaking. Chhaya's issue had crept into that.

She could have kept it a secret. What would be her condition now? The future has been marred, hasn't it? It's a type of suicide. Our town is defamed. Mohangarh would mean the place where the house of a teacher called Chhaya is situated. Lo, the new identity of our town!

She has great stamina. In that dishevelled body and tattered attire, she was in the Police Station and Hospital. I couldn't believe my ears at first. I have been seeing her right from her childhood. She appeared quite calm and innocent. I say, she appeared; mark it. Who knew what was there in her? Why did a gang of loafers fall upon her? Such a thing was never heard before.

Listen, you are doing harm to her by praising her saying that she has stamina and courage. Where do her courage and stamina land her? Are her businessmen brothers able to walk keeping their heads high? They look frightened and insulted while talking with someone. Her father frequented the shop earlier but the old man is hardly seen these days. Chhaya has been finished, destroying her entire family. What would you call her- inauspicious or a bad omen?

That was not so surprising a comment. The people would have reacted to her precisely in the same way no matter whatever Chhaya had done. Amiya could not grasp if there was any place for the rape victims in the world or in the heart of man. Did she mar her own future? Could it be called suicide? Painful though, Amiya thought that assessment of Chhaya's future was unmistakable perhaps. Poor Chhaya! A shrilling current passed through his body. Ah, Chhaya! This time his legs and hands started to quiver. He asked for another cup of tea.

Leaving the shop under the care of the two helpers Tushar came near his motorbike. Neither did he say where he was going nor when he would return. He did not tell it to Pravir or to any member of the family that he was going to the office of the D.I to try for Chhaya's transfer to a convenient school nearby. Father was not regular in coming to the shop. After the event, he did not go out of the house for some days.

That incident had become a spicy topic for gossip in the street. After ten or twelve days, people waited for a far more exciting incident. For them, defamation was a prime matter of discussion for their entertainment. Incidents- big or small took place everywhere. After a few days, they were erased from memory. There was no fun in that.

Chhaya was recovering fast. The wounds had healed up leaving the scars. Visible or inconspicuous—scars would linger.

A zero watt bulb lighted her room. The struggle

against a non-existential terror was not there as it was before for the first few sleepless nights. She was smartly active in helping her mother and sister-in-law in household chores.

No one in the family ever raised anything related to the incident for discussion. Although it was very important a matter; Chhaya could make it insignificant. If there had been too many things like wailing,   squealing and head-crashing to express the grief, the people would have availed it as good stuff of entertainment for long.

Tushar had never asked if Chhaya wanted a transfer to some other place instead of going back to that school. She had the need for a transfer. She could never go to her old school. Could she stay in Atanu's house or anyone else's? There was no house in the village strong enough to ensure guarantee, safety and security to Chhaya or to any other member.

The family had made a silent agreement with Chhaya's future. The possibility of her going to someone's house as a daughter-in-law had been lost. She had a job. That would be the only support and consolation for her. She would spend the time in the school oblivious of sorrows, sighs and seclusion. She was in service and while in service she had been raped. She had the job and had the strength of confronting the worst eventuality of the rape too. She had to be posted at a convenient place nearby so that she could be reached immediately as and when wished. Everyone in the family would rest assured that she remained secure within the range of their sight.

Chhaya might object to Tushar's going to the D.I's with the argument that she was not prepared to leave the school for her fear of someone. Why would she escape? Or it might so happen that she would accept the transfer order to another school to get peace. Tushar was not sure as to what would be Chhaya's reaction. Only for that reason he had not disclosed where and what for he was going.

He had heard that the D.I was not a man who could be easily approached. Such animals were everywhere. Many teachers trembled when his name was mentioned. He would never look at anyone or sign any paper without a bribe. Non-demanding officers are not taking birth anymore in this holy land of gods.

Anticipating less rush, Tushar reached the D.I's office about 4 o' clock in the afternoon. Without taking any permission for entry to his office, he got into his chamber. A man wearing a sobbing face stood beside the D.I's table with folded hands. The mighty seated in a throne called chair was almost rebuking him. He did not come to school regularly. Whenever he came to school he thrashed the children without any rhyme or reason.

The explanations came in a feeble voice that allegations were not true. The Head Master was involved in politics and would never come to school. The Head Master got dissatisfied as he brought the matter to the notice of the village chief. He had been threatening to put him in trouble by writing against him to higher authorities.

The officer kept sitting silently without being aware of the presence of Tushar in the least. His face so appeared as if the entire education system had collapsed and the responsibility to set it right had been entrusted to him. How far a single man could go! He was put to a lot of pestering problems, and there was no one to think about his difficulties.

: "What happened?" The utterly disgusted and dissatisfied officer focussed his grumpy look on his table after throwing a moment's glance at Tushar indicating thereby that he had the least interest to know about Tushar's problem.

: "Sir, I am Chhaya's brother." Tushar had never been so polite to anyone before, not even to the Sales Tax or Commercial Tax officers.

: "Chhaya? Which Chhaya?" He would go on asking while browsing the pages of a file.

: "Sir Chhaya; I mean the incident that took place ten or twelve days back." Tushar had no words to introduce Chhaya.

: "Oh, yes." He was electrified as it were. This time he looked not at the file but at Tushar and went on blurting out, "Why does she sit at home filing an application? New job and she is on long leave! There is a hue and cry all over the state that there is no teaching in the schools. Tell her to go to school tomorrow; do you understand?"

Tushar's muscles were tense in a trice; the mercury rose up as if all the blood of his body rushed into his brain. His grips were tight. Tushar was in search of the culprits to give vent to his anger and take revenge.

He had not found them. The man sitting before him in the chair seemed to have impersonated all the criminals. But, Tushar controlled himself.

: "The doctor has advised a month's rest for her." Of course, Tushar's anger could not outdo his humility. He said, "Sir, we had sent an attested copy of the medical advice to you."

: "I don't know," The D.I said. The doctor would say one thing, and the school needs another thing. Sundry people ask me why there is no teaching. The teachers are running to the doctor on the slightest pretext, and the doctor would very happily advise them to take rest at home, and not to move. To what extent can I solve the matter?"

What would Tushar do? Would he smash the egoistic heartless officer with a single blow? It wouldn't take a minute's time for that, but he still had tolerance and forbearance in him. This time he said with the same humility, "It would be challenging for Chhaya to continue in that school. Sir, I request you kindly adjust her in a suitable place so that she would commute from home. She gets frightened at the thought of staying in a rented house."

It was as if a plunderer located the hidden treasure of a miser. The miser wouldn't be as cautious as the D.I had been to have heard the appeal for a transfer to a suitable place. "Suitable place! Would I manufacture a place like that? No one would go to distant places. In that case, will the Government close all those schools? Has the doctor told this also that there would be no recovery without the transfer to a nearby school? Go, go; don't waste my time. There would be no transfer-like thing at present." He looked down again on to the table.

: "Your head will break into chunks." Coming closer Tushar told him in an undertone. His warning did not end there. He muttered, "Your head would break in such a way that the doctor can't repair it. Your legs and hands will not remain as such. I can do this but don't provoke me to do that. Now, what have you to say? Tell me whether my sister will be transferred to a suitable place or not."

The D.I looked miserably helpless. He was not in a position of attacking others. He looked like a tamed snake going into its basket.

Tushar was not in a mood to enjoy that state of him. He said, "Chhaya's posting will be in some school situated in a radius of maximum three Kilometres. Any school at a distance of seven to eight Kilometres having bus communication would also do. There are so many options before you. Learn to help the people in distress. Then only you will fare well and remain safe. I will come to take Chhaya's transfer order just after ten days, at 4 o'clock on Tuesday, the 22nd of this month."

Then he stood straight, said, "Namaskar" and came out from the office.

Life did not stop at that day's mishap. To confine herself for fear of shame and insult was far from reality for Chhaya. Instead, she would do all the household chores and would go round the colony. She would go to the market even when there was no need for it and would spend time in Tushar's shop at times.

Though no one in the family appreciated her going out like that, there was no open opposition to that. The scar marks on her body gave her a new identity. She was bent upon making them trifle and insignificant. She had not escaped to another world after the rape. Why would she? She was very much in the mainstream,and there was no line to separate her from that nor had there been any in the past either.

Chhaya's power and determination were amazing. She could withstand a heavy blow without shedding tears and without feeling shrunken or insulted. She was much above any one's sneers and sympathy. Her reaction to the circumstances seemed remarkably matured and seasoned.

She was at a loss that the culprits could not be caught. Possibly, there was no willingness or earnestness for that. Then why did she go to the Police Station in a half-dead state bearing the pangs of uncountable wounds? That was not a mere obstinacy. She did not consider that a blind and stupid step. A number of important things were concerned with that but the outcome was nil. She took it to be a frustration a few days ago. Her sentiments were severely wounded.

Then she did not feel like that. The culprits and the police moved in their respective ways. The victim, without getting any justice, was also on her way. There was no punishment for the culprits, no justice for the victim. It was awful, yet there had been no difficulty for Chhaya to live the life. The wristwatch had been out of order. A known shopkeeper had repaired it. The gold bangle on her left hand had been deformed and the one of the right hand was lost in that fretful night. The jeweller had made a new pair.

She bought sarees and *bindis,* used them with much love and interest. She walked along the road, moved around the markets. Taking the looks of the people as irrelevant and unimportant she proclaimed her presence saying, as it were, "I am, was and will remain known as Chhaya. This world, the land, water and air belong to me; the dust of the road and the depth of the sky are also mine. By the grace of God, I have a job, I will spend my earning, and I will achieve the things I deserve."

: "Take, here it is." Coming back in the evening Tushar handed over a piece of paper to Chhaya and asked his wife, "A first-class tea please."

: "What paper is this? Chhaya asked while unfolding it. A bird's eye view of the paper delighted her. There was a mixture of pleasure and surprise in her tone. "You must have gone to the office of the D.I. Nothing happens there *suo moto or suosponte.* Why? You hadn't told me about your going there."

: "I hadn't." Tushar admitted and lifted the cup. He said, "I thought you would object to my going there. I didn't like that you would go again to your old school. Of course,

I had to threaten the D.I. However, you have not been transferred to an inconvenient place."

: "Not at all." She looked satisfied. Chandanpur! It suddenly occurred to her that journalist Amiya belonged to that place. She asked, "How far is Chandanpur from here?"

: "Ten Kilometres. There was no vacancy in any school within a radius of three or four Kilometres. Chandanpur School is near the bus stop. It is ten minutes' bus journey from here. Somehow you manage a year there; next year you will be here in this town." Tushar said confidently.

Chhaya had not told anyone in the family that she was going to the Police Station. She would make a querry about the status of her case. She knew it pretty well that nothing would happen. Her FIR would be lost among other unnecessary papers like an irrelevant piece of paper. But she would go to the Police Station to let them know that she had not forgotten about her FIR. She still had the same concern for that; and that she had not changed her mind after filing the FIR or had not thought it immaterial if the Police did not take any step.

The rest was the fiery speech of a teacher in front of the hospital, a warning to paralyze the entire education system if the culprits were not arrested within a few days.

Such speeches create temporary excitement in others. The listener for a few moments goes above the limits of the self; he broadens and identifies himself with the one undergoing pain and oppression. He protests against this and cries for its abolition and for an uninterrupted happy life of man. The fiery speech gives birth to such psychology.

Everything subsides in due course of time bringing relief to man. Anyway, neither has he nor anyone of his family been ill-fated with suffering and atrocities. However,

he has existed without losing anything. He salutes God-
"My good God, how merciful you are! The other fellow
suffered and got lost. Of course, it is unfortunate, but I am
alright. I progress. Let this good grace of yours be on me
forever."

Everyone moves in their own way. Time passes on.
Sometimes it stops at the occasional cry of someone in
agony. Pathos arouses fear in man's mind at all times for
the same misfortune might befall him. No one stops; his
journey continues.

: "Where are you to so early? It's not nine yet."
Gananath asked. Chhaya would not take her bath at that
time ordinarily.

: "Father, I am going to the Police Station." As usual,
she was very polite, affectionate and persuasive.

Gananath's face looked sourly though he had been
overwhelmed by an intimate feeling. He said, "My dear,
why should you go there? You won't get anything. Don't
you know this? Rather you would feel better if you
compromised with it. You withstood the slings of such
outrageous misfortune and stood straight proving
yourself superior to that terrible ordeal. All cannot do
that. That is enough for us. Don't revisit the old wound,
dear."

That was not only a piece of advice of her father; that
was an appeal instead. Of course, Chhaya was prepared to
hear something like this. She said, "Father, I am not going
to the police to beg. I haven't any doubt that the police
have not given any importance to my FIR. I still give the
same importance to my FIR. I am going there just to remind
this. They may avoid me; they may even insult me. Just to
cover up their inefficiency they may treat me harshly. It's
immaterial. I am prepared for that. Father, don't refrain

me from doing that, please. It is only an hour's distance by bus. I will be back by lunchtime."

Father could not say anything anymore. He felt at times that Chhaya was growing larger. She had started advancing step by step towards her determined and delimited goal. She would give its justification when asked. She did not seem illogical. He, finding her ready to leave, said, "Why will you go alone? It will be better if Tushar or Pravir accompanies you."

Chhaya smiled and said, "Is it that big a thing? Why should I trouble them unnecessarily?"

It was half-past ten by the time Chhaya reached there. The Officer-in-charge stood on the veranda and was blurting out something in a slightly excited pitch to the people standing below. He saw Chhaya wishing him. Contracting the brows he tried to remember where he had seen her.

The officer came down. Scarcely had he taken two or three quick steps when the *havildar* informed, "Sir, your phone. The M.L.A. wants to talk to you."

Faster than before, he rushed up to the receiver. He used the words, "Sir and Yes Sir" very liberally with utmost humility. He would say assuring him that he had nothing to worry till he continued there. He would work keeping his orders and interests in mind.

Replacing the receiver, he wiped his face with his palms. He laughed to himself recollecting something. While leaving the chair, he saw Chhaya.

: "How now?" He gave an oblique hint that he did not appreciate her coming there.

: "I am not sure if you could recognize me." She smiled with all politeness. She gave an impression that she would not be hurt or offended if he could not recognize her.

: "Oh no," the officer emphasized as if obliging Chhaya. "Who said I could not recognize you? You are, after all, an unforgettable personality."

Chhaya was surprised to have heard such an equivocal adjective from him, yet there had been no change in her face. She said, "Sir, I came here just to know the progress in my case."

The officer shrank a bit. Looking to both sides twice or thrice he said in the manner of convincing her, "See, we are trying to arrest the criminals. The real problem is that the rascals have not left any clues. Besides, many serious cases are being reported from the area under my jurisdiction round the clock. We are running here and there. We are overburdened."

: "My matter is no less serious." Her tone was firm without any excitement. The officer remembered how Chhaya had beaten him in argument a month ago. He felt it difficult to admit that Chhaya had some specialty in her personality.

: "Who said it's not serious?" His statement seemed lacking any spirit. He continued, "Sometimes, it takes months, even years to arrest the criminals. Doesn't it?" He meant the challenge at Chhaya.

: "Yes." She had to say.

: "Then?" The officer said without allowing her any chance to speak, "Yours is a fresh one, a few days old. I said we have been trying. There's no use worrying."

: "Sir, I want to say that there are instances of criminals being arrested within a few minutes of something happening." Chhaya did not want to show any tension. But there was the mark of it. She asked, "Aren't I right?"

It took no time for anger and insult to occupy the

officer's face. He felt uneasy. He said, "You go now. Could you hear me? I said, "Please go." Don't destroy our sympathy for you. I am not bound to say anything about the progress of our inquiry."

Chhaya was about to burst into laughter to have seen his mood, but she realized that there might be an explosive situation if she laughed or said anything more. She reached home by one o' clock. She changed and refreshed herself. But nobody at home asked about what had happened at the Police Station.

Chhaya undertook another expedition before she had joined Chandanpur School. It had been past ten by the time she reached the District Headquarters after travelling a distance of forty Kilometres. She knew from the Rickshaw puller that the S.P's office was almost two Kilometres away from the bus stand.

The S.P was in the office. The havildar sitting at the door said that a meeting was going on inside and he did not know when it would be over. Chhaya might send the slip after the meeting. If the Sahib agreed, she could go into his office.

There was a small crowd. People generally gather at places like this. A thing comes to mind at the sight of Hospital and Police Station that man is in some health-related problems. Man is entangled in one issue or the other everywhere-in the temples, at the bus stands and stations. Chhaya sat on a bench. She looked into her repaired watch but could not know the time. She wiped her face and waited, the meeting continued. She had accumulated the patience to go on sitting like that. Therefore, she was not impatient or tossed up.

The door opened after an hour. Chhaya had given the slip to the Havildar. She had marked 'Rape Victim' under her name. This information might prompt the Sahib to allow her an interview.

She was astonished when the havildar said that the Sahib waited for her.

She went in, saluted him. She was asked to take the seat before him. The Sahib was in a civil dress. He was a young man. He was grave but did not look like discouraging anyone to speak.

Chhaya took a piece of paper out of her bag and said, "This is the carbon copy of the FIR I have submitted. It is over a month the incident of rape took place. Reaching the Police Station the next day I filed the FIR. At that time my condition was very miserable, Sir. Countless injuries were there in the entire body, and there was terrible bleeding. It was not easy to walk or talk. The police came to the spot and said that it was the mischief of some young men of the village. Till now there has been no progress in the case. I met the Officer-in-charge two days ago. He told me that it takes years to arrest the culprits and mine was only a month old."

The S.P went through the paper. Following his direction, a clerk connected the Officer-in-charge. The S.P expressed his disgust over the undesirable delay and ordered the arrest of criminals forthwith. He said further that it was a very sensitive issue. If the culprits were not taken to task, people would lose confidence in the police and the rape victims would not come to the Police Station to lodge an FIR.

He asked to call the stenographer. No sooner did he come than the S.P gave the dictation. That letter would be dispatched to the Officer-in-charge to expedite the inquiry.

Chhaya felt relieved when leaving the office. The police had a sympathetic humanistic element. She should not lose her confidence. Perhaps there would be some pleasant tidings shortly.

She would go to the Bus Stand. There were some rickshaws outside the office compound. A car slowed down near her and stopped before she had proceeded to hire a rickshaw. A PRESS sticker stuck to its window screen.

Amiya was before her the next moment asking, "You, how come you are in the SP's office!"

Chhaya would not have been that delighted if she had seen anyone other than Amiya. She was preparing to give him a brief account. "Let's do one thing," proposed more intimate and smarter looking Amiya. He said, "I have only fifteen minutes' work here for which there is an appointment. I am free after that. I have no other work for the day. Please come and sit for a while on the veranda. We will talk after the work is over."

Amiya did not give her any scope for objection. Chhaya had no mind also to object to that. She would return home soon. All at home would be anxious for her. Chhaya forgot that. By the time she sat on the bench, Amiya had already got into the office.

Amiya came out in less than fifteen minutes looking satisfied which was an evidence of his success. His smile broadened to see Chhaya again. He asked her to come with him.

They came up to the car. Amiya gave another proposal: "I have to go to a village via your town. I won't get the chance to have my lunch en route. Let's have our lunch in a good hotel here. We will have chitchat, and by the time I leave you at your house we would have finished chit-chatting."

At this point, Chhaya stepped back. If she went by bus then, she would be at home by the lunchtime. She had also told her mother to keep her food in case there was any delay in her return. She shrank within at the thought of going to a hotel with him for taking lunch.

: "Why will you take the pain for me?" Chhaya said. There was a tinge of intimacy in her tone. She said, "I can return comfortably by bus. They must be waiting for me at home."

: "I have no doubt about that." Amiya said. He, in fact, had not finished. He said, "I want to get some information about you. Pausing a while with a good smile, he said, "I have not forgotten about your story for our Weekly. Please come with me; I am not the sort of person to put you in trouble."

The car entered the gate of the Hotel Ambassador and stopped at the parking. Arranging for the driver at the Reception, Amiya stepped on the stairs and urged upon a hesitating Chhaya to come with him. The A.C dining hall bathed in a silky soft light mixed with soothing music. Some people sat there waiting, and some were enjoying their lunch.

: "Would you like to go to the washroom? It is there, go and freshen up. You will feel comfortable."

While giving orders, Amiya said, "Are you a vegetarian? What a pleasant coincidence! I too am a complete vegetarian.

: "I will join in Chandanpur School after a day or two. I have been transferred to that school." Chhaya said as if she was giving some information to him.

Would he be delighted or worried for she might be in difficulty? Amiya could not decide. He said, "It is ten Kilometres from your house. Of course, there will be no problem as there is bus communication. Perhaps you will commute daily, won't you? I belong to that place; I suppose you remember."

: "Yes," was Chhaya's brief reply.

Chhaya narrated everything while taking the meal. She felt relieved after presenting a complete detail.

: "I don't think both the verbal and written order will be effective." Amiya said. After a brief pause, he asked, "Are you prepared to bear all this?"

: "You know what I have withstood and how prepared I am to bear further. Chhaya was neither boasting nor greeting herself. She said, "I did that much perhaps for my own satisfaction. I could console myself that I could do that what I ought to have done. I have not thought about its result. In fact, I pay no importance to that."

Never before had Amiya met such a lady. The lady teacher of the Middle School seemed extraordinarily straightforward and pure. Amiya was over flooded with love and regards for her. What a beautiful metamorphosis of the wounded and bruised body! He was almost bathing in the sweetness of Chhaya's personality.

: "Then why can't you do another thing?" Amiya said laughing.

: "Is there anything more that could be done? " Chhaya expressed ignorance, "What is that?"

They had finished their lunch by that time. Amiya advised, "Wait for a few days. If nothing comes out, take shelter in the court of the Judicial Magistrate or the Sub-Divisional Judicial Magistrate."

Chhaya's face brightened. She looked encouraged and eager. There was still a way before her. She became effusive for that reason. She said, "Really? Can this be done that way? Can the Magistrate order the police to carry out investigation quickly?"

But Amiya did not participate in her enthusiasm or effusiveness. He said, "Do you think such a directive will do magic? There will be that same conventional reply. The search is going on; we have not captured the culprit yet; not a clue even."

Amiya was sorry that a fresh flower would fade away on hearing that. He said, "I am not at all encouraging you to do something like this. The entire thing is crystal clear. Why will you break your head against the wall of inaction and non-cooperation? You came to the S.P; that is enough. Doing anything after that would be nothing but madness." Such things could only be told to one closely related.

The car moved along the uneven road. Both of them looked ahead. But, Chhaya had paused at the old episode. She was running from pillar to post to get justice for herself. She had not yet acquired that. Possibly, she would not. What could it be called- her personal failure or the indifference of the system set for the society? This system was a hollow but dazzling placard. It was visible, but it was devoid of voice. Who knows, perhaps the system for some reason or other had not addressed her issue. But she would take the last resort. She would go to the Judicial Magistrate as Amiya had advised.

: "You look very serious." Amiya remarked.

: "Is the matter not serious?" Chhaya returned.

: "No doubt! Very serious," he conceded and asked, "You want the culprits to be identified, and you are prepared to put in the last effort. You say that the result of the effort will neither make you happy nor unhappy. When I said, you might get answers like 'we are searching for but not getting the criminals, or have no clues' you could not conceal your disappointment. Am I right?"

: "Yes, you are." Chhaya agreed. She said, "Efforts are made to achieve something. Man feels defeated if the desired result is not accomplished. It is justified to think like that. If at all the culprits were arrested it would have been a message to the society that crime yields punishment. People would have faith in the system, and I would have got satisfaction. Things would not happen that way. That would not be a loss to me as there could be no greater loss for me. What would people think about the system? Just imagine how the culprits would congratulate themselves.

Amiya did not say anything for a long time. Some years' journalistic life had taught him one thing. All the institutions meant for organising the people and to foster their creativity have been rendered paralytic, corrupt and ineffective. Except for a heap of cheap and verbose excitement in the name of democracy nothing good happens. The people of this country are engulfed by sheer deception.

Their bodies shook as the car moved on. Amiya felt drowsy. He became conscious hearing, "Would you have some water?" Chhaya's water bottle was before him. He had some water. Chhaya also drank some water and kept the bottle in her bag.

: "What will you do? Amiya asked. His next question was, "Will you approach the Judicial Magistrate?"

: "Sure!" Her voice had a firmness that Amiya appreciated. Chhaya said, "I will knock at every door of possibility; however fruitless it may be. I had been alone, most alone and helpless at the time of rape. This is no less a state of loneliness. The door of possibility is not opening. Can the inquiring officer look straight to my face easily after all this? Surely, he will be ashamed and will feel guilty."

Amiya could not control himself; he laughed. He thought for the first time that Chhaya had been immature in certain aspects. She thought about the ethical norms only.

: "You laughed? Why? Did I say anything wrong?" asked Chhaya being surprised. She looked naive; and therefore, beautiful.

: "What will he be ashamed of?" Amiya said in a slightly angry tone. He said, "There lies the problem in this country of ours. Shame has become old-fashioned for the employees. Many, nay, most of them care a fig for disgrace or defamation. There is a frequent abortion of justice. No one thinks himself guilty. Repentance and guilty consciousness are getting lost as irrelevant and obsolete. You will know when you will mature with experience whether what I am telling is true or false."

There was a long silence as Amiya was under deep drowsiness. Chhaya's cogitation was clear and at work. She looked once or twice at Amiya. She didn't like to disturb him.

Taking the final leave of his drowsiness, Amiya asked, "Do you know any advocate practicing in the court of the Judicial Magistrate?"

: "No." Chhaya said giving an indication that would not be an issue with her.

Amiya scribed something on a piece of paper. Handing it over to her he said, "This advocate is known to me; he knows to plead. I may also write a letter to him about your problem."

:"Thank you!" She said after a glance over the piece of paper. "Thank you for your concern for me." She begged of Amiya's permission through her tiny smile.

: "I don't encourage you exactly for this." Amiya said. He made himself clear as he apprehended the possibility of offending Chhaya, "You will knock at the door of this possibility if the SP's directions did not yield anything good. I am just helping you. You will have the satisfaction that you did whatever you ought to have done. Your satisfaction will also be my happiness."

Chhaya felt the vibration of a sensation. At least for a moment, she had the feeling that she was not a total void within. She was not alone perhaps. Someone else would be delighted at her satisfaction! How reliable was it? What sincerity was there in that affirmation? She could not assess it but a current of love and regards for Amiya ran through her.

This touch was of a different nature. The appeal of this touch she had never had here-to before. This, with profoundly intimate warmth, made an excursion all over her mangled nerves. This was a sure solace for her dwindling, deterring and lonely existence. It was beyond Chhaya's perception if Amiya's statement had his emotional approval. None the less; the immediate effect of the heard version was the blind acceptance of it; the analysis and determination of the veracity of which takes place at a later time. Amiya would not also know how Chhaya had been grateful to him for some moments.

The car stopped in front of her house. While getting down, she said, "Would you not step into our house? Last time you left without having a cup of tea even. Should you go back like that this time also?"

She was very humble like she was before. It was not easy to avoid such a cordial and polite request. If avoided; it would amount to hurting the sentiments of a dear one.

: "Come." Amiya said and got off the car. He sat in a chair in the passage hall. Switching on the fan, Chhaya went in.

Mother and vouja were at home. Chhaya came back with a jug and glass. Amiya might wash his face if he chose and might drink a little water. He took some water and said with a smile that it was relishing.

The clanging of bangles at the door announced the presence of her mother or vouja with tea.

Amiya took tea. He looked serious and thoughtful. Chhaya stood leaning against the wall in front. She enjoyed watching Amiya take tea at hers. Amiya said, "After two or three days your story will be flashed in our Newspaper. You had to approach the SP against police inaction. It is expected that both his written and verbal order would yield some good result. This message would be there in the story."

He looked at Chhaya and asked, "What do you say? Should we publish such news?"

: "OK. Go on. Publish." There was not that much interest in her voice.

: "Good." Amiya expressed his satisfaction. This time looking with a smile at Chhaya he said, "You had not encouraged my interest in making a story for our Weekly a month ago." Chhaya did not say anything. Her smile broadened. Amiya got up saying, "All my sincere and good wishes are for you! Oh, yes, tender my regards to father and mother please."

He got into the car waving his hand. Turning back, while crossing the passage hall Chhaya saw mother standing nearby. There were clear signs of dissatisfaction and resentment written on her face. Chhaya thought of giving some explanation. She would clarify at a later time about her coming with Amiya by car and having undesirable relation with him. She felt that it was not the right time for that. She behaved in such a manner as if her relation with Amiya was not worth discussing.

But no, nothing happened like that. Towards eight at

night after half an hour after his return, father sent for her to the passage hall.

: "Ma- who is that man? He came straight to the topic.

: "He is a journalist. Detail report of the incident will be published in their Newspaper. He is from Chandanpur. I will join tomorrow in his village school."

He seemed bit relieved. But the worried and upset father said, "Since you are working, you will have to mix with many. You don't know their intention and their attitude to you after the incident. You will have to be very cautious in these respects. You will not do any such thing to allow others to take undue advantage of that. You returned with this gentleman. Those who have seen it will not take it in the right spirit."

Such concern and apprehension are entirely justified. Chhaya had not been hurt for that reason. Chhaya expressed everything clearly- right from her first meeting with Amiya till her accompanying him by a car that day.

She said further, "Father, I have been much cautious after that night's ordeal. I won't do any such thing that would reflect on the prestige of this family. Perhaps, there won't be any mistake in knowing the people. I won't do any stupid thing after anyone 's temptations. I will feel good if this much confidence is there on me."

Her father kept quiet. It's not known to what extent he relied upon her affirmations. But, one thing- others' discussion about Chhaya and their sneering at him, perturbed him. It would be there. The rapid development of their family economy was sure to arouse jealousy and intolerance in others. The people were looking for loopholes in the family. There was no difficulty for others to pick it out. Chhaya was the suppurating lesion of that family. Chhaya! Her family is an object of easy ridicule! She stayed there; the most sensitive part of the family lay exposed. That could be easily outraged. Chhaya stayed there!

: "Should I accompany you to the school?" Pravir asked her at 8 in the morning. Chhaya was preparing to join in the new school. The road and the Bus Stop were at a stone's throw. The bus takes very little time to reach Chandanpur. The school was situated beside the road at the centre of the town. Chhaya assured them that there would be no difficulty in joining. Pravir did not insist on accompanying her. Father, mother and the elder brother Tushar- no one was worried for Chhaya could do it alone. In the meanwhile, she had been to different places and had returned safely.

The bus arrived around 9, a few minutes after she had reached the Bus Stand. She had to struggle with some other passengers to get on the bus; the helper of the bus was not helping her for sure. He had intended to place his hand on her back. Not only of this bus but the helpers and conductors of all buses invariably did this with women passengers. The body contact with a woman! Matter does not end there. Even some passengers in a packed bus crave for a touch. Chhaya's experience revealed that no exasperation, no hauling nor any red-eye could get rid of such a wild craving.

Like all bus stands Chandanpur Bus Stand also had a small market. The specialty of this market was its fresh vegetables as the villages in the periphery grew them abundantly; the tea and pan stalls were there just as they were in every bus stand.

There had been no problem in matters of her joining. The Head Master and other teachers including the primary school teachers had known Chhaya although some of them had not seen her. There was no unpleasant curiosity; she marked an ardour for showing sympathy and extending a helping hand, instead. Within a brief time of half an hour Chhaya had said to herself that it was her school; its pupils and the colleagues- all belonged to her. The floor from which the cement plaster was getting off; and the soaking wall acquiring various patterns belonged to her as well. There would be no fatigue, no boredom. This job was the only support for sustenance. She has no other ambition, no other discontentment either. All her zeal and concentration confluence here for this school only.

Although it was her first day at the school, she went to the classroom. She gave a unique, loving look at the students which affirmed that Chhaya had enough patience and stamina to teach standing before the students. She loved that job. That was her potentiality, her forte. She had been made for teaching. Teaching was her identity, her definition, her passion, and the desired destination.

Chhaya had never expected to meet Amiya at the Bus Stand the next day. She was not aware of the people's gaze at her. She did not feel shy. She had been overwhelmed to see Amiya there. She thought that no one had been there or anywhere to see them or to mark the pleasant emotion writ on their faces. It seemed as if all had withdrawn themselves to allow Amiya and Chhaya the entire stage.

: "How come, you are here!" She had not known what to say at that time though she knew it pretty well that she had to pay a 'namaskar' to him.

: "I belong to this place."

Amiya proved his presence as natural. As a welcome note, there was a delightful smile on his face for receiving Chhaya in his village. Amiya said, "Keep this paper with you, and this is from my behalf, and this is from the villagers' behalf some gifts for you."

Amiya handed over two ballpoint pens to her hypnotized hands. This type of pen was not in much use at that time. Chhaya had not imagined that she had to adapt the ballpoint pen as a substitute for the fountain pen.

Even at that place, there was a thrill, a captivating rhythm in the blood flow and a humming of sweet melody in the ear. Chhaya knew that there ought to be some sort of soft resentment at the time of accepting such gifts. That resentment often took the shape of gratitude. She had no such words for that. Before she said something, Amiya said, "We had been to a hotel that day after coming from the SP's. I had marked that three fingers of your right hand were stained with ink. The fountain pen paints such pictures on fingers at times."

Perhaps there would be no recession of the spellbound state. Thus she would go on sitting under the hold of a melodious hangover. Why did she want to be under such a trance? She was trying the two pens having a blue and red refill on a piece of paper. Scarcely did she know that she had written Amiya's name for so many times on that paper. Perplexed, she woke up when she felt that the hand that held the pen had been under the spell of Amiya's hand which controlled the movement of her hand. She was only under his unseen guidance.

Why was there such a pulsation within her? A word of caution came out to her which was also a type of touch. The first work of this touch was to defunct the preventing faculty of one through an unhindered sweet persuasion. Being hypnotized, the person would enter the cage of cajolery. Its passion would have taken over in the meanwhile the person's thinking power and process. The person under the trance would get transformed into a defenseless entity.

Ultimately, the person would have to submit to the intention of the one that gave the touch.

Then there would be no need of holding the hands or shutting the mouth. There would be no necessity of concealing one's identity in the darkness. Wasn't it Prof. Chandan who had done like that? The urge for getting this touch becomes so violent that one becomes restless and mad. Who would care for the consequence at that moment? For one without the sense of discrimination, the touch becomes the only truth. The fire blazes on within with all its flying fury. To quench it, one needs touch after touch, many touches like that.

: "Have you not had any lesson yet?" The ball pen stopped. Chhaya came back to herself.

There was a sense of defiance in her. She said, "Was it forbidden to have good relation with someone?" She liked Amiya. Amiya was good indeed!

There was a roar of laughter in her. Was it only good relation? Was that all? Nothing else more than that?

Chhaya gave a retreat. She recollected the Newspaper; unfolded it. It was about the order of the SP to arrest the culprits forthwith. The report was not that satisfactory. It would have been better if there had been no such report. Would it expedite the police action to catch the criminals?

But, brother Tushar became reactive at home. "What would come out of it? Better it was buried. The media aggravated the issue unnecessarily by publicizing it. Again Chhaya was at the centre of criticism. It was awfully unpleasant."

A month's time had elapsed in the meanwhile. She had not met Amiya. Chhaya would be wonderstruck when such anxiety to see him and hear him rose up within. She would not give any threat to such anxiety. The question, 'who Amiya was to her', could not raise its head.

To her utter delightful excitement, a letter was there for her in the school address. How are you? Hope, you must like our school etc. etc. Nothing was there in the language, yet there was thrill behind the words. It had not been difficult for Chhaya to mark that. Amiya had not written for a reply but had given his address in it. That indicated the then psychograph of Amiya.

Chhaya had written back in a restrained manner. She wanted to approach the Judicial Magistrate. She had with her the advocate's name Amiya had given her. She would file the petition through him. And then she would try to forget that she had ever fallen prey to rape. If there were no criminals, it had been a sheer nightmare then.

Amiya had replied to her letter. Chhaya would be at the advocate's by 12 on Sunday. He would be waiting there for her. The court would summon for an appearance at a later date.

Chhaya had made it known to the family members before the appointed Sunday where and why she was going there and who had to help her in that respect.

There was a flash of bitter disgust on the faces of Father, Mother and Tushar. Chhaya did not know how so much of dislike for her came into the mind of Tushar. The love and sympathy for the younger sister were no more there with him. He also could not give vent to his feelings. He would get easily excited and lose his temper. He left the place for he did not like to present him in that mood. Father and mother were there; let them face it.

Gananath had no patience. He said, "We are not able to assess what you want. The news came out in the Newspaper a few days back. We didn't like it. And now you would go to the Magistrate. Why do you want always to be in the news? Stay comfortable at home, leaving all these. I see that you don't want to accept my advice. And as for Amiya, it would be better for you to keep a distance from him."

Father wanted to remain aloof from her activities. Maybe at a later time, he might say- "Chhaya? Who is she? We don't know her. Our family has nothing to do with her."

Mother tried to convince her. She said, "You have not broken down after such a big calamity. Still, you keep your head high. It's a matter of great pleasure for us. But we do not like your stubbornness in keeping the issue alive. We are worried about that. Stay at home; go to school and come back safely. Don't keep any relation with Amiya or anyone else. It is dangerous for it may lead to defamation. We are under great tension for you." She started sobbing, wiped her tears with the corner of her saree.

Father said ultimately, "Can you not do this much for the sake of the family?"

It was a sort of very powerful appeal by her father. Her determination to fight got slightly shaken. What should she do? Should she not proceed in the matter any further? As Amiya said, it was not right to expect that it would yield a good result. Was it wise to break the head against a stone-wall made with the mortar of inaction and indifference?

But that very work was the last of its kind for the road ahead ended in a blind. Chhaya would be settled and would lead a normal life. She only said that. "Why should I want to be in the news? Can I ever want the disgrace and insult to this family? Give me this chance only. There would be satisfaction for me that I did whatever had been there to be done. I would not bother about its result. Amiya is my well-wisher, and that is the base of the relation with him. I know him very well. I trust him."

Gananath left the place without giving any comment. Her mother sat leaning against the wall, heaving sighs and looking elsewhere.

She had no difficulty in getting the advocate's house. Amiya had already been there. Chhaya was delighted and grateful. She was yet to know where she had come- to the advocate or to Amiya. In fact, it had been secondary whether the advocate would write the petition or not. Meeting with Amiya was a great thing for her.

It was a friendly atmosphere there. Chhaya signed in the form. The advocate said that madam's statements would be recorded in the chamber of the Magistrate as the matter was very sensitive. Basing on that the directive would be issued to the police station. There was absolutely no complicacy in that. He appreciated Chhaya's courage and determination.

He became slightly disappointed and said, "You took the matter to this stage. It's a great thing. But the Magistrate would not search the miscreants since that work is to be done by the police. What they always have is the usual answer-search is going on; the case will be registered as soon as the criminals are arrested."

Despite Chhaya's objection, they had lunch at the advocate's.

Chhaya heard that she had been afraid of- 'Come; let me drop you at your home.'

: "No, no, don't do like that, please." She shrank.

: "They will object. You are afraid of this, aren't you?" Amiya said with a generous smile. He wasn't interested to confound Chhaya. He said, "Alright, I will explain everything to them, Okay?"

It was at this point that Chhaya got frightened. But she found no way to give a check to Amiya. She said, "Please leave me at our Bus Stand; I can go easily from there."

Chhaya was caught here, but Amiya did not comment on that. Both of them got into the Press car. Chhaya was ill at ease; she could not feel normal and cheerful. To conceal that she asked, "How come; you used the press car for this?"

: "Not at all." Amiya said adding, "Today I had to meet some local gentries here. For my own convenience only I had told you to meet the advocate today."

There had been not much conversation. Chhaya could not feel the vibrating emotion like she had done before. She could not enjoy the presence of Amiya either.

Amiya could understand Chhaya's mercurial mental state. Poor girl!

But the car did not stop at the Bus Stand. Following Amiya's wishes, the car moved on and was soon parked before Gananath's house. At that time Father, angry and resentful, stood at the door. Chhaya marked that and got angry within. She went into the house hastily without inviting Amiya to come in.

Amiya got out of the car smilingly. Saluting Gananath he was about to enter the house. Gananath prevented, "I have a word with you; wait there."

But Ganannath was astounded as Amiya did not wait outside. Almost avoiding him, Amiya entered the room and sat on the chair. His smile defied the anger reddening Gananath's face. Amiya, as if enjoying a good sport said, "Definitely I will hear you; but please don't take it amiss for I am telling about my issue before that." Then as a mark of showing courtesy to a guest, he said, "Please sit in that chair. I will take a minute only."

Amiya's behaviour seemed freaky. By that time, however, Gananath's temper had cooled down a bit. He appeared slightly stupid and confused. Like an obedient boy, he sat in the chair and looked at Amiya.

: "If you have no objection, I will marry Chhaya. Amiya said adding immediately, "Of course, I haven't sought the opinion of Chhaya; I don't know if she would agree."

Not only stupidity; skepticism had also shrouded Gananath's face. He was not sure if he heard him correctly. Perplexed, he looked here and there. Licking his lips after a good pause, he asked in a feeble voice, "What did you say? I could not hear you exactly."

: "I am not married." He continued like giving testimony, "I have no bad habits. I have lost my parents since long. In a way, I worship my brother and sister-in-law. However, much before his expiry father had separated us. I have some landed property in Chandanpur. Though not a very good one, I have a house and I work for a Newspaper. I do not get a very high salary."

His smile disappeared for he had submitted himself and was waiting for the verdict of the judge. Never before had the room held such silent suspense; quiet and stunned! Not a stir was there or anywhere. Swallowing the saliva and licking the lips Gananath wiped his face with the towel he had on his shoulder. He then looked straight at Amiya's face.

: "You know everything about Chhaya." It was not easy for Gananath to articulate the words as his mouth had been parched. He would have been full of thanks if someone had handed him a glass of water. He said again, "Why do you, being an educated and earning young man want to marry her? What would your acquaintances think of it?"

: "I don't deem it necessary to think about them."

Amiya affirmed, and with the same firmness, he continued, "They may admire me and may also sneer at my back for some days. For the last few days, I have been observing Chhaya, and I have been delightfully impressed by her personality. I have been attracted and overwhelmed by her audacity to be in face to face with life and her confidence and power to assert herself. I mixed with her for the last many days with the only intention that she should know me well so that such proposal would not give her any shock, nor it would take her by surprise."

Once again language got itself lost in the wilderness. Gananath went in without saying anything. A few moments later Amiya became aware of two faces under the veils looking at him from a distance. Amiya's identity and position for that house had changed already. There was curiosity enough to see him as if he was altogether a new appearance.

Gananath came out and said, "I will consult with my sons."

Amiya was alone in the room; the clanging of distant bangles reached his ears. There was the faint sign of movement. Then Amiya would cast a new look at the room that seemed intimate. At the next moment he thought of going in just to say, "A cup of tea, please!"

Though slightly bored, Amiya felt very light. What if no one agreed to his proposal! Would Chhaya reject it also? What was next then? How would be the life devoid of Chhaya? His intimacy with Chhaya and her presence in the very thought and blood of Amiya shook his entire being. He stood at the end point of patience. Would he go in and holding Chhaya's hand say, "Come with me, your place is there with and within me; care a fig for their damn negative rulings. I know how deeply you love me."

Almost after fifteen minutes or so, Tushar and Pravir were there with Gananath. "Yes!" To only say this much, the two were there leaving behind their business; to say this much only, they held up all the household business.

There would be no procession, no party nothing of the sort. The marriage would be solemnized in a temple in the presence of a few. "Do you have any objection? Chhaya would come to me with no presents but only clothes." Amiya said.

They looked at each other. "Yes," Gananath said on behalf of all.

: "Please allow me a minute to have a talk with Chhaya," Amiya appealed.

Chhaya entered in slow steps; looked at Amiya. Her eyes became wet, and tears rolled down.

: "I will come on any day. Trust me; it's no acting." Amiya got out.

Only a few days later she was Mrs. Chhaya, Amiya's wife! Unprecedented and unbelievable! It was the talk of Chandanpur town to the shock of many.

Couldn't he get anyone else? Why with so much secrecy- was there any mystery there? No such incident had occurred in that area; there was a wide discussion everywhere.

: "What? Amiya is at home having married Chhaya in the temple!" His elder brother could not decide whether he would laugh it out or accept it as true. Looking at his wife, he said, "Hey, do you hear- you loved this brother-in-law of yours so intensely. Now see,what he did. He didn't even drop us a hint!"

He was about to go out of the house in lungi and vest to verify the authenticity of the news.

"Wait, why are you going like that? His wife searched for the conch and the puja plate. Only after ten minutes she, along with a few housewives of the neighbourhood, was there at Amiya's house situated at distance of a hundred meters.

Showing the lamp and blowing of conch they adored them with their warbles. Vouja hugged Chhaya. That was the recognition of the family.

: "Why did you do like that?" Abhaya complained with utter disgust after the small celebration had been over. You didn't take even us to your confidence."

: "None of you would support me." Amiya admitted with all humility. He said, "I would have married Chhaya even without your approval. And that would have been a sheer insult to you."

They spent an hour or two there. There had been a party for all villagers preceded by some rituals.

FOUR

Chhaya sat down-faced resting her head on the knees bound by her two hands. She was mulling over the time present and the betraying past that tossed her in a sea of hopes and despair. Amiya also sat there quite close to her. There was none in the silent room except the soft, silent, soothing blue light spying over them.

Breaking the silence, Amiya said, "Chhaya!"

Overwhelmed Chhaya raised her head slightly.

"Look here Chhaya, I have a lot of things to tell you but the night is too short for that. I have been waiting eagerly for one like you to listen to me. See Chhaya, from this very moment, I am yours; you have undisputed ownership over me. All that I have is yours-the house, the landed property and its income. You can use them the way you like." He was abnormally loquacious as if possessed by some unseen power. "Since I work in the town, my uncle and aunt are living in this house. They are issueless. By and by you will feel how affectionate and loving they are. I am always a small child before them. They control me with "why did you do that; do that way" like things. Chhaya, I love to hear their guardian like advice. At times, I feel that they are fountain heads of inexhaustible love and affection which they want to share with the entire world. The couple scarcely feel issueless as they treat all as their sons and daughters. Isn't it great? They have been here much before my father died. You will find no problem due to them.

Chhaya looked at him.

Don't worry, I will take you to my place of work, but it will take some time to arrange for that. I think of leaving the present job as I have a plan to become a freelance journalist for which, I am adequately equipped with a good command over English and Odia. Although I am fond of reading literature, I have no hesitation saying that I lack the talent of a creative writer. That is no issue for a freelancer. Then you will be my only boss.

Chhaya smiled with a how-lucky-I am-look.

Believe me, I had a great desire to get you; I had no craving for any other thing. I am contented with my lot. I enjoy the simplest food like wet rice with tamarind as much as the delicious dishes served in star hotels. I am never a foodie; you have nothing to worry for that. I am a very simple man; I enjoy the company of the greengrocer and the betel seller as much as I can be with great sorts like ministers and top-ranking officers to take their interview. Amiya was unfolding himself.

Taking some water from the glass he continued-

See, you have full liberty as to how you would teach in the school and mix with the people of the village. My brother, sister-in-law, uncle and aunt are there with you for the time being. I do not like to repeat about how broad and helping natured they are. You can give the full play to your creativity till you haven't left for the city. I know your firmness and determination would control every move of yours to work out a final definition of your destination. As I told you, there are four guardians to guide and advise you. Of course, you are more mature than your age for you have seen much of the world and studied human nature. I have not marked any childish fickleness in you. This house, this village and this world, all belong to you. Have them all with pleasure. The broader and expanded you are, the better and prosperous will be our life. Be happy dear; exploit the possible scopes of happiness; and adopt yourself to that.

Are you going to finish everything in a night? Won't you keep anything for other nights? Chhaya said.

: Feeling drowsy or bored?

: Oh, no! Not at all; I wish the night to continue without an end.

Just a second Chhaya, let me not hide it from you that a moment's instinct has not drawn me to you. I had the eagerness of getting you after much and prolonged mulling over. I will treasure the joy of getting you forever. Never, at no moment will you think that I have obliged you by marrying you. You were and will be there in my heart. You are the answer to my curiosity, the end of my quest! Now I am in love with this village, its dirt and dust, the poor houses and even with the ridicules shot at us. Never before did this world seem so charming and beautiful!

Of course, I don't deny the existence of treachery, jealousy, intolerance, anger, and violence in the village. Nonetheless, there is love; there is sympathy and an extended hand to embrace others. The gong of the temple bells, the aroma of the incense, the beat of the *mridangam* and the warble of women are there as well.

It was a sweet and soothing sermon to her as it were. Chhaya listened to it with rapt attention. She wondered if it came from a nearby place; or from Amiya who sat very close to her. It appeared to her that the sweet and soothing things descended from a world of sanctity and serenity of which she had no idea before.

Everything seemed empty and wordless after Amiya

had finished. At the core of that emptiness and wordlessness pervaded an indefinable buzz there in Chhaya's consciousness as well as in the air of the entire room. It created an ecstasy resembling the sweet stream of nectar oozing out of the chanting of OM.

Amiya cupped his hands and held her face affectionately within it. He saw that her face was washed off with tears and the tear brightened by the joy of triumph was the language of her heart. No one was prepared to wipe it.

Chhaya looked at the exalted face of Amiya. She said, "I don't know if I am worthy of your trust and confidence. Honestly, I haven't seen the world nor have I met life. Whatever I have done till now has been inspired by my inner being. Neither have I the knowledge nor the power to adjudge its propriety. Here before your feet do I surrender all the flaws and follies and all the shortcomings; and my total self. You are my saviour; you are my salvation, my identity, my existence, my love, my life and my journey's end; in reality I am nothing.

Amiya laughed.

Chhaya could not know why Amiya laughed like that. Pray, don't take it for a joke. She said.

: No. I don't take it that way; rather I feel elated to get a soul mate like you. How beautifully you express humility!

: You are no less a magician of words; how nicely you tell the good things! Chhaya came closer.

And then there was the touch. Chhaya had never got the feel of such a warm, fulfilling and trustworthy touch. As if the variously-touched body of hers had kept something reserved to capture that ecstatic experience! A halo circled her despite the darkness. The command of that touch was what she desired the most at that engrossed moment. There was an air of rhapsody that presupposed no danger since it was filled with a lot of promises. Amiya looked up to keep that state of ecstatic stillness in his hold.

They had a house and some landed property; the land that lay open and unidentified behind the house needed demarcation. Both of them had jobs that made them self-reliant. Not only that, uncle and aunty were there. Elder brother Abhay and appa too were there at a little distance. By what name other than affluence would it be called? Such unexpected gifts and good fortunes! What could it be if not the grace of God? Misfortunes befell in everybody's life but they at times opened doors to something good. She was the proof and a burning case in point.

She marked within that short time that Uncle and Aunty had been feeling restricted. In a way, they had withdrawn themselves. Their helpless looks at her resembled a feeling of indebtedness as if her generosity had given them shelter. They would leave that house without any demur at a small cue of her to only embrace helplessness bereft of shelter. It was the first thing for Chhaya to remove that notion from their head. She had to create the confidence in uncle and aunt in a very subtle manner like that the house belonged to them too so that they would feel free and comfortable. Gradually and unconsciously they would be attached to this house very intimately and would be their guardians as before. She thought of adopting ways like- 'Aunty I feel very hungry; let us eat together'; or else like- 'you have cold; you go and take rest; I will wash the utensils'. Or even like- 'Is uncle going to market? There is my purse in the bag. Oh, why do you show me the purse? Take as much money you want. Please buy a towel for you.'

Although Abhay Bhai was a man of few words there

was no difficulty in feeling his love and affection. In the true sense, he was an elder brother; never did he give the impression that he was Chhaya's *dedhashura*. He had a very loving and intimate voice. As a caring elder brother he said "We need to put up a hedge around the plot behind the house; I will arrange the labourers. It's a very large plot. Have you seen it? What did you say, you will plant trees? Very good! Perhaps you don't know uncle and aunt can work hard,but they can't apply the brain. I see; you have already marked it then? But take it from me, they are very innocent and honest to the backbone. They will do as you say."

Appa, Abhay Bhai's wife, remained a bit depressed. It had been three or four years since their marriage, but she hadn't any children. So much of fasting and rituals, worship and prayer in the temple had yielded no fruit. She had been obsessed with an apprehension. She said, "Will you also do *sudashabrata;* do you have the book? Wow, it's a very good thing. Did father bring the book for you? Why didn't you tell him to come to our house? You should have. What if he stayed for an hour there? He could have spent at least five minutes at ours."

Within a few months, Chhaya commanded love and respect of all. But in the beginning comments and questions like 'What, don't you know anything about the teacher Chhaya? Why did you ask if you had known it? She is a famous lady. We took Amiya for an educated and competent young man. What did he see in that teacher that he brought her home marrying her secretly? She looks very calm and gentle but lo- how she trapped Amiya. She must be a professional. Had it not been so, how could a gang fell on her at night? How tactfully she trapped poor Amiya within a month or two after the incident!'- were in the air.

It was Chhaya. None before her had taught so well. To the best of our knowledge, no teacher loved the children so much. We hadn't ever heard a teacher hugging and kissing a child doing well in the class. Who before her had the patience to tutor a dull student and to infuse courage and confidence in him to make him feel that he had the potentiality of doing well?

Chhaya soon transformed into Chhaya madam- a reputed personality of Chandanpur.

Amiya was more overwhelmed than astonished to see the hedge around the plot of land. Wasn't it a magical touch that defined the land? At present, the house did not look morose, lonely and abandoned or out of the way. He went around it. A lump of clay was going to be transformed into an earthen image.

: "Of course it looks very nice. This should have been done much earlier, and you know better now why it couldn't be done earlier," Amiya said.

: Yes, but I have marked with what interest and pleasure they helped the workers. *Bhai* was telling the right thing- the two had no brain to do something of their own.

: "True, they haven't the brain." Amiya got up wiping his legs and hands after washing them in cold water. He said, "Now the house begins to look like a hermitage. But how long do you think of staying here? Should I be a lifetime guest of the hotel and have to sweep my room forever?"

Taking the towel from Amiya, she said that her suitcase would be instantly ready the moment he asked her to go with him but for that the house and land should not be neglected.

Amiya became serious. It would take some time to post Chhaya in any school there. He could not know if

Chhaya was happy there. Did her smile and happy look speak of her enjoyable and pleasant stay there?

Perhaps Amiya was telling his vouja about his plan of transferring Chhaya to any school in or around the place of his work. This was somehow spread in the village and the school. The children surrounded her in a manner of creating a fortification around her. They wanted to make it so thick that the transfer order would never penetrate through. Everyone looked moron; they were about to burst into tears.

"Would you go leaving us behind? What mistake have we committed? Punish us; never shall we make any noise in the class. We will come prepared to the class with all our homework. If you left, who would teach us like you?"

It was very pathetic a scene. Chhaya was moved and overwhelmed due to such touchy gestures. She had only taught them with great interest, loved them and encouraged them to do still better. This is quite normal on the part of a teacher; she could not know if there was anything special about that. But the reaction the children showed apprehending her transfer made one thing clear. In the process of teaching, she perhaps added and shared something unknowingly. And that strengthened the impulsive bond between them. They were just protesting the possibility of separation.

Such devotion to the profession within such a small span of a few months! There was enough cause and justification to be exalted and overwhelmed. None the less, how could she be indifferent to the needs of Amiya? She was prepared to go to Amiya at any time. The children would get a substitute which was not possible in the case of Amiya.

Some ten to twelve villagers came to see Amiya that evening. Most of them were elder to him.

: Amiya, are you there?

Amiya was surprised to see them. While he thought of giving them seats, they had already sat on the floor. The elderly priest spoke in the manner of accusing him, "You are the most educated boy in our village. You are working in a Newspaper office, and you are busy there. You hardly get time to come to the village. But, after our daughter-in-law came here, we see you here."

He continued after taking a pause, "Have you ever done anything for the village or for the children of the village?"

Amiya looked defeated at such direct attack on him. He was confounded; his smile dimmed pitiably. He said, "Uncle, I didn't have enough time as the work claimed all my twenty-four hours. You, all the guardians of the village, tell me what you wish me to do. I will try to carry out your orders."

This time another said, "You say you would carry out orders but, in fact, you have already attempted to destroy the school."

Amiya could not figure it out. A cousin explained the situation, "Amiya bhai, we heard that you are trying to take vouja to your place of work."

After this whatever they said appeared jumbled up. "There was no good teaching in the school; the teachers were not regular. The children of the village were going astray. Leave aside English and Mathematics, they were very dull in other subjects also. Our daughter-in-law has been teaching well. Our vouja knows the difficulties of each and every child and tries to solve them, etc. etc."

: "Why do you shout like that? The priest cried out

impatiently with disgust. After some time all kept quiet. The priest said, "We will go to the office of the D.I to file our petition. The daughter-in-law of our village will continue teaching in our school. Her husband can also never take her from here. He would manage as he used to before his marriage. Our daughter-in-law will stay with us."

Amiya had never expected to hear this. He did not think it a small achievement on the part of Chhaya to be so indispensable for the village, that too within such a short time. He was overwhelmed again.

: "What happened? Why are you not saying anything?" said another.

: "Since you repose so much of confidence in your daughter-in-law, she will stay here but she has to go to me for a day or two intermittently. If I leave the job, the situation might change." Amiya said.

Someone from among them said, "Leave the job at the Newspaper."

They returned after a long time, satisfied that there was no immediate possibility of her applying for a transfer. They were sceptical whether she would continue to stay there forever.

Amiya had been justifiably overjoyed for that reason. He had marked the utmost devotion in Chhaya not only for her profession but for the family. He had no idea that Chhaya had been able to create a place for her in the hearts of the villagers.

Amiya was in high spirits.

: "My advocate friend has sent some information to me." Amiya said explaining what this information was. "You had appealed at the court of the Magistrate; the date has been fixed. The court is going to summon you soon."

Chhaya became serious. She looked gloomy. She

seemed a thing that tried frantically to free itself from a painfully unpleasant mesh.

: "Is it possible to withdraw the complaint?" Chhaya said.

: "Why not?" Amiya was slightly delighted. He said, "As such the Magistrates are awfully hard pressed for an excessive overload of cases. If someone for some reason withdrew the case, the magistrates ought to be happy."

Amiya did not like the expression that Chhaya's countenance bore at that time. He could guess under what mental state Chhaya was at that moment. He tried to lighten it saying, "You withdraw because you think that the culprits would go scot-free, don't you?"

Chhaya heaved a sigh keeping the fixing of a button in Amiya's shirt pending. She said, "I had been for the second time to the officer-in-charge. You know I had also approached the SP. The hope that the criminals would be caught and would be taken to task had already faded then."

: "Then what made you go here and there against the desire of your family members?" There was a surprise in Amiya's voice.

: "I would have certainly appeared before the Magistrate if I had not married. Chhaya emphasized. And I have also told you before that it would have been a consolation for me for having done whatever I ought to have done."

She resumed fixing the button, looked at the needle and finished her explanation saying, "Now I need no such consolation. A far greater achievement has already come to me. This family, the school and the people of the village and that I am a housewife are more than enough for my identity. I do not want to revisit my misfortune anymore."

: "Then should I inform it to my advocate friend accordingly?" Amiya asked.

: "Yes." Chhaya said. She concentrated on fixing the button. Her dissent for any further discussion had been apparent.

They spent most of the Sundays in the small rented house of Amiya. During the long vacation, the house in the village remained under the care of uncle and aunty. After a bus- journey of fifty Kilometres, one has to hire a rickshaw to reach Amiya's residence. It had two small rooms, a bathroom and a kitchen. It is very likely that Amiya would not be at home by the time Chhaya reached there.

She would open the rooms with the duplicate keys she kept with her. She would clean and set right the house at sixes and sevens and do a lot of things like washing the floor with phenyl water, bleaching the toilet, cleaning the gas stove and brushing off the soot, changing the pillow cover and bed sheet. That would take almost an hour.

A cup of tea was most relishing after she had a bath and changed her clothes. Then she would spend some time watching the newly bought TV. After that, she would take out of her bag different types of homemade cakes of Amiya's choice along with the things like rice, pulses and turmeric powder, the fruits, and some vegetable grown by her to store them in the cupboard.

The small rented house was not too far from the Newspaper office. Before marriage, Amiya stayed in a mess. He took this house on rent so that he would live there with Chhaya. For the last few days, the eagerness to bring Chhaya to that place had diminished slightly. Of late, he would not speak of becoming a freelancer. No good salary was there for journalists although the job claimed much time and labour. Chhaya knew nothing about his lack of interest for the organization.

Normally, not more than a two-three days' comfortable stay in that rented house was possible; as during that period, she would keep herself busy in every bit of work beginning from cleaning the house and clothes to cooking.

After that, she would feel like going back to the wide-open ambiance of Chandanpur. There she would move freely and comfortably in her house, courtyard and in the large backyard to get the pleasure of observing the plants grow. Besides gossiping with uncle and aunty, there were Abhay bhai and appa, the school and her students and the colleagues.

Reaching his residence at about half-past eight, Amiya had to knock at the door several times. It was enough to get an idea that Chhaya had fallen asleep. The door opened after a little while. As usual, an affectionate gleam born of his generous smile was there in his face. The dinner was over with queries and responses like if she found any problem in reaching there; how bhai, vouja and the uncle and aunty were; and if labourers were available for working in the field. Their chatting would continue till late in the night; till one of them fell asleep while listening to or speaking to the other.

By seven o'clock in the morning on Sunday they had been ready to visit the gynaecologist for which Amiya had got an appointment.

Chhaya saw for the first time such a large number of expecting mothers at the doctor's residence. Some of them were serious, almost apprehensive. Some others did not look like they were going to be mothers. They belonged to different age groups who came there with various other problems. Chhaya was one among them. She too had her own dream like that of others. The process of creation was in a mystery.

Does it create a thrill, an eagerness to get something? Does the identity change after having the good fortune of being a mother? Is there any gratitude for such power for creativity?

Chhaya's turn came not after an hour or two but after almost three and half an hours' tedious tarrying. The waiting time lingered in such a way that it came to her mind that the rest of the months would pass on in waiting only before the mystery unravelled itself.

: "Did the doctor say about any problem? Amiya wanted to be sure.

: "No," was her brief reply while getting on the rickshaw.

: "He must have said something." Amiya was impatiently anxious.

: "He said everything is normal and there was nothing to worry." But Chhaya was somehow looking serious.

: "Then why do you look so worried?" Amiya's voice was slightly agitated.

: "Tell me, what way I look worried." This time Chhaya smiled a little.

: "Has he not advised for rest?"

: "From now? Really, what a mad man you are!" Chhaya laughed at Amiya's ignorance. She said, "I was thinking about appa." She seemed morose. Amiya did not think it proper to say anything more.

For the first time, Chhaya had disobeyed Amiya. Why would she go to the town for delivery when there was everyone in the village to look after her? Moreover, there was no apprehension of any sort.

And without any problem a son was born. A year

later Sony came to Abhay bhai's world. Appa had some serious problem before the delivery. There was acute labour pain. Luckily a jeep was available to shift her to the hospital.

: "The village people can't pressurize us anymore." Amiya was relieved and confident. He had come to the village for the naming ceremony of his son Kim. Amiya was elated to see Kim. In a manner of making an announcement he said, "He would stay in the town with us and would be admitted in the best school there. Enough of teaching in the village, let's see to ourselves henceforward. What do you say? Of course, I haven't much faith in you. In the first place, you become suffocated there in that small house."

: "A lie!" Chhaya protested. She asked, "Have I ever said I didn't like the house?"

: "Is there any need of it?" Amiya was light. Again as if recollecting something he said, "In the second place, the people here have made you their dearest one. Haven't they? It is no small achievement of yours. It's not that I wasn't pleased about that. But now I say it's enough. Our son will stay with us and study there. That's final."

Final! Kim would study in the town. No compromise was acceptable for Amiya. Was that final?

Which of the things was final for Chhaya? Then how was that the words and the breath of the man announcing it came to an end? What was the final?

Accompanied by Abhay and appa, Chhaya reached the hospital with her four-year-old son Kim. It was past midnight. This was that man, nay, it was the body of the man who had succumbed to a motorcycle accident.

Chhaya, with all her wounded thoughts, kept on gaping like an idiot. Who was he? She could not have answered it. Where was he? She could not have heard this question. For her, the entire world had turned to a corpse. Broken bones, shattered muscles, and the drained blood! The motionless heap under the cover of a white sheet was Chhaya's world, detached and unconcerned with the present and future. All crushed to a big nothingness. That was the shape and form of her old world. It was a disposable thing of no use! Therefore, not on bed but on the floor was laid her broken world.

At this age, if Chhaya was asked, "What did you see in the hospital? What was your feeling at that vacant moment? How much tear did you shed?" She would give a sad look at the person asking such questions. She would cast such a glance as if the question was not worth answering. Was she really there in the hospital that she would have thought, seen or have shed tears? Such things are destined to have no tears at the time of courting them. The sense-body cannot perceive it as there is no touch anymore.

It was not at that time alone. Nothing could she know- how the cold, motionless and silent body was loaded in the car, how it was transferred on to the bamboo bier and put at last on a pyre, a bed of firewood. Did anyone think that Amiya would be burnt in a wheel of fire and would be converted to a heap of ash or would be lost in the air in a moment's time?

When after the funeral rites Chhaya madam went to school, heart rending lamentations and countless sighs would greet her on the way. It seemed as if the air and the atmosphere had been overcharged by a stirring strain of pathos. The firmament descended close to ask her, "Are you Chhaya? And to say, "I had to come down to you for it was difficult to recognize you from a distance." Stunned and petrified was everything- the grass, the tree, and the dust. They affirmed that she was none but Chhaya for only a Chhaya could walk like that twelve days after what happened to her. They said, "We know you well."

The lamentable pathetic change of her appearance shook the Head Master and all the assistant teachers. The mettle that held her was perhaps lost or weakened. Chhaya looked like a disconnected electric bulb that had lost every possibility of reconnection. She seemed very lonely and helpless.

: "Madam, we were there." He said with a touch of empathy looking at other teachers, "We could have managed your classes. There was absolutely no problem. You should have taken rest for some days more."

It would have been better if she had not beamed. It made her face more miserable. She said, "Sir I know, you are prepared to help me in this way also. How long should have I stayed at home? Rather, I would feel better to be in the midst of you and the children. That house is an incomprehensible void for me. I met discomfiture everywhere there."

She went to the classroom. Albeit their tender age, the children knew the gravity of her calamity. Smiles had fled from their faces. That touched Chhaya madam. She tried to smile. Holding the book, she started to explain. She was like a musical instrument out of tune and out of harmony not willing to create a symphony. But after a few moments, the instrument activated itself.

There was symphony mixed with unseen sharpness which gave a new life to her teaching.

: "If you agree, I could get you transferred to our school within a few days." Not only Tushar, but younger brother Pravir had also given that proposal, not once but many times.

: "Where would I go leaving this house and property?"
Chhaya said. After a small pause she said, "If father and
mother see me, their heart will break into a thousand pieces.
I face no problem here. You two are there. At the time of
need, I will seek your assistance. This confidence would
give me strength and energy,"

But there was a chill in the house. Everything in it
wore a weeping face- the growing plants in the spacious
backyard, the flowers seemed like blooming against their
will and showed no interest to share their fragrance. The
hay recently thatched looked depressed; dejected was the
served plate of rice and the hearth with its fire extinguished.

Had there been no Kim, it would never have been
easy for her to face life. His presence had already defeated
the pang of separation within a period of five to six years.
Her world remained stable even amid the absence of Amiya.
Although belated, there wasn't any difficulty to understand
that the orbits of the Sun and Moon are predetermined;
the wind blows; the trees and plants grow, and life goes on.
Like them she had to carry on.

She went for a new television, planned for a good
house and went on dreaming about Kim who was not good
at studies; the dreams never came to an end.

Sometimes the dream was shattered as nightmares
encroached upon its place. Chhaya realized that it was all
vain to become ambitious about Kim for he was not worthy
of it. Chhaya could not see any such possibility or promise
in him; no smack of it! He was too poor at studies. It was
not difficult for her to accept it. She had no role in making
him intelligent or unintelligent; no one else had it either.
But he could be humble and obedient and could remain
within the expected limits.

He would create problems; his conduct reflected

disregard and defiance. Chhaya asked to herself if Kim was the greatest failure of her life, and the cruellest ridicule to her.

'Disobedient and inattentive' was the common remark of the primary school teachers about Kim. Kim was under her direct supervision. She would teach him and explain the things to him when all on a sudden Kim would begin to be ill at ease and irritated. He would say- let this much be for today; let me have some water. Sometimes, he would gape at madam's face without any reaction. Hey, what happened? Could you not understand it? Such questions would not touch him while he would keep on sitting like that.

Chhaya was almost exhausted; she was at the end of her nerves. Suppressing the disgust, she would say lovingly- look here; I explain it once again. Why don't you listen? Slightly agitated she would shake him by the shoulder as if his concentration was fixed elsewhere; a shake would perhaps bring it back. Kim would yawn untimely just to indicate that it was better for her to do some other work at home instead of wasting her time and labour like that. His open mouth showed only a big void. It was so big a void that Chhaya's teaching got lost there being unable to put a single dot there.

She felt vanquished and utterly helpless time and again. Her inability to improve a kid like Kim and his non-cooperation aroused anger in her. The anger remained unventilated within her for which she would burst into tears standing at a corner of her bedroom. The failure was not hers alone; it was of Kim's also. The child understood nothing; he would say, "I want to watch the TV; why do you switch it off? Is it for this you bought the TV?"

: "What did you say to the Mathematics teacher in the class?" Chhaya was not in a mood of excusing him.

Kim had not been familiar with such gesture of his mother. He fixed his look at her while unbuttoning the shirt. Then he was about to leave the room throwing a suggestion that her question was entirely irrelevant and unimportant.

Chhaya fell upon him. All her blood rushed up on to her face. Despite that she controlled herself and asked, "Was it right to tell the teacher that way, dear? He is your teacher, you know. How could you say so in the class; 'why are you chattering unnecessarily like that?' Think for a while what a bad thing you told him."

Trying to get out of her clutch he replied without any repentance, "He is like that always; talks a lot."

The next moment Chhaya lost control over herself. Her faculty of discrimination and judgment got lost in the fire of fury. Her hand was raised at Kim inadvertently. Aunty rushed in first, followed by uncle to save the boy. They protested shouting, "Will you kill the boy? Is it for that you begot him?"

This punishment had a surprising impact on Kim who was in class five then. He stood without any fear or crying except that his face had turned red. His hair was in shambles. He kept on looking at his mother. Nothing significant has happened; why was mother so wild? Possibly for this, he pitied his mother through that look.

And that frightened Chhaya. What was that boy- terribly stubborn, unruly, untameable, uncivil or all these and many more? Chhaya was at her wit's end. There was a feeble ray of hope if he became attentive and devoted himself to his studies. He might not do very well, but he could reach the average standard at least. That did not happen. Kim would derive pleasure abstaining himself from studies. He would make his teachers aggrieved and hurt by his rude and indecent behaviour.

That night clasping Kim's face on her breast she entreated, "Promise me, you will never say such things to the teachers and will be attentive at your studies. Promise."

: "Yes," said a hesitating voice.

: "What does it mean? Chhaya asked affectionately.

: "I won't say bad things and will be attentive at studies."

Was there any sincerity in it? Chhaya was not in a condition of analyzing it as if she had been gifted with a boon. Elated she kissed Kim's cheeks and forehead. Kim sat without any protest. Chhaya for the first time saw the light of hope, feeble though. She asked, "Will you apologize the teacher?"

: "Yes, I would." Amen again.

The light named hope would get extinguished at times; again it would show up itself at a remote place near the hazy horizon. Chhaya would think it not to be the light of hope but a daydream. The light was a mental illusion only. What could be done? Verbal warfare with someone at play, attacking someone with the cricket bat or ridiculing some senior persons—Chhaya had to go to their houses three or four times a month to apologize for all this. Caressing the head of one injured by Kim, she would assure— Kim would not do like this in future.

An aggrieved elder said, "We all know what a good person you are. No one can teach like you. Only this has been safeguarding the boy till today. You say you are trying to keep him under control. Is it called control? He is not a small boy, when will he be disciplined?"

Sony, younger than Kim by one year who was in class nine said to Chhaya, "Aunty, Kim bhai has shown bad behaviour to a girl. She could not share it with anyone out of shame. She told it to me. She said, "I worship Chhaya madam. Tell her, there would be a very unpleasant situation if Kim did any such nuisance with her again."

Chhaya could not say anything for some moments. She waited for the violent wave of anger and insult rising from her toe to the tip to subside. Though not a brilliant student, Sony was known for her humility, sense of responsibility and a capacity for compassion. Chhaya often hugged Sony when she saw her smiling. While showering on Sony her love and affection which she could not give to her son Kim, she would ponder that Sony also belonged to her family. If she were her daughter!

: "It must be true." Chhaya said. For some time she felt undone to do or say something. Heaving a sigh, she said, "What shall I do now?"

: "Aunty, I am very much pained to see Kim bhai's style of conversation, dealing and conduct." Sony was really pained. She said, "Shame keeps my head down. You are trying your utmost to discipline him, but it is of no avail." Sony's voice was soaked with sympathy.

It was past five by the time Kim returned from school. Chhaya would mark him while he was changing his dress. An attractive white complexioned perfect body with dense curly hair looked bigger than his age. He had been putting on full pants since the previous year. He had shining shoes and beautiful socks. He looked different from others. He was much concerned about his appearance. He spent much time before the mirror. He would not tolerate slightly shabby pants and shirts. His shoes ought to be always shining.

: "Your classmate Sushama's father and brother had come." Chhaya took to a lie. "They have given a warning." She was stacking Kim's dresses on the rack.

: "Which Sushama?" Kim expressed ignorance. He

by that time had put on the trousers. His other question was, "Why did they warn you?"

Both her hands were tense. The muscles got up to attack. Her face was heated due to the violent circulation of blood; often it happened with her like that. Tension would mount when darkness would envelope the entire universe, and then her consciousness would get lost in a tremendous throb within the head; as if some stuffed and restless matter would go off.

Kim's presence and the complaints against him created in her great anger. All her nerves and the blood cells would become brisk and alert. Some unpleasant and undesirable thing might come off the explosion of anger. Self-control was necessary to give a check to it.

The way Kim asked these two questions made Chhaya blind for some time. She controlled herself with much difficulty. That possibly provided Kim with an element of entertainment. Chhaya looked at him with a censuring eye. 'Rascal and arrogant,' she muttered. Then she said, "You should be aware of what Sushama's father and brother could do. I have told them that the brat is not under my control. You could do what you deem fit."

It had no impact on Kim. He moved for washing his hands and legs in the courtyard. Chhaya asked, "Do you understand anything?"

: "You know how to make others understand; you have a good name for that." Kim wanted to hurt her. He was successful in his attempts. He was about to go out of the room.

: "What did you say; do you know me?" Chhaya could never say; how she shook Kim's shoulder rushing at him out of an acute and frantic fury.

Kim glared undauntedly at her. He smiled a little and gave a mysterious answer; "I hadn't; now I begin to do that."

No one can say what explosive the reply was stuffed with. Its meaning was not clearly understood; although the two hands of Chhaya had dropped down from Kim's shoulders. Infirm and benumbed, she stood motionless for some moments and saw absent-mindedly that Kim was washing in the courtyard. Like a machine, she rushed into the kitchen. Kim would be hungry; there should be no delay in serving the food.

Kim had not known her, and was doing then. She was Kim's mother. Was there any identity of her other than this? Was Kim unhappy and ashamed and hesitated to give her the mother's position? Was it painful and intolerable for him to bear the burden of insult for being her son?

She could not muster the courage to ask what he meant by "I hadn't; now I begin to do that." What would be there in her life if Kim said that? There would be an avalanche within her, and her world would come to its end. Chhaya was never so afraid before.

But how could the dark day of the past remain a secret? Chhaya had expected Kim to be sympathetic towards her and to accept her naturally as his mother. She would then narrate the horrible story of that inauspicious terrible night to him. She would describe frankly without any shame with what eagerness she had struggled to identify the culprits.

Nothing like that happened there. Kim perhaps knew about the incident. It was a different thing how correctly he knew that. But of late, he had become a rebel and was asking her, "What made you to bring me into the world? How can I walk keeping my head high with dignity? With what identity shall I live amid the masses in the world?"

A new building was being constructed. She failed to comprehend how she, in her split and anxiety-ridden state of mind, could keep the record of the brick, sand, and cement along with other building materials supplied from time to time. As such, she also could not feel the grief due to the recent death of uncle and aunty. She was there, yet at the same time was not there or anywhere. Never had she been separated from the classroom. That was the source of solace for her. She had not been separated from Kim either. He was her greatest attainment and emotional support.

Of late, she felt alone and alienated; most painfully abandoned and rejected. What of a house in such a state and what was its type? To what extent would it fill up the void in her? What type of living and what sort of love for life was there after being irrelevant and unwanted?

But these two amazing things took place, and the lost hope and future plans seemed to get a new life.

First- Kim passed the Matriculation anyhow; even though his mark sheet had not overwhelmed Chhaya. Second; and the most important of all—no complaint of any sort against Kim reached her. He looked serious and depressed as if there had been no space available in his face for a laugh. Joy and happiness found there no place as well.

Kim would feel for himself. Perhaps he became conscious that he hadn't a good place for him anywhere even in his own circle. He spent most of his time at home watching TV and browsing the Newspaper and the pages of books. All these were for a brief time. Restlessness and helplessness had their clear marks on him. He went to a newly opened college at a distance of ten kilometers from home. He knew well the way to the college but would not find any road to his future. In fact, he had not been keen on finding it out. He would go to the college as he had no other work to do at home and as boys came to such a place after matriculation.

He had been to his uncles' after passing the plus-two examination. Never before had he had any interest in going there, although they would send for him time and again. Kim had to go there as it was not possible to avoid their repeated invitations.

Four days later he returned, after being the owner of a motorbike and a cell phone. Chhaya was taken aback to see Kim getting down from a motorcycle. She looked askance at him. She had the apprehension that Kim had committed something somewhere.

: "Uncle gave it." Kim announced with unbound joy and gratitude. And taking the cell phone out of his pocket said, "Look, this also!"

Chhaya was not so happy for her capable brothers had presented those two things to Kim. She became elated and fidgety for the way Kim expressed his joy. It was absolutely spontaneous. It was altogether a different issue whether Kim got back his mother or Chhaya got back Kim after so many years.

: "It looks wonderful." She said to keep his joy undisrupted.

: "Uncle said, 'it had been bought for you." Kim said. Chhaya became over delighted.

"Her Kim looked handsome and attractive!" She mused.

Kim had no grievance or grudge against anyone who would stand on his path of pleasure. He had never been so loquacious. He added further, "Uncle said, there ought to be a vehicle to serve at the time of need. Your mother might need to go somewhere; you would help her in that."

Kim stood before her. He wanted to drop the hint

that he was ready to take his mother around the world. "Tell me, if you want to go anywhere. Maybe, you doubt my ability over biking. But I have already become an expert." He prided and created confidence in Chhaya's mind.

That was an unbelievable and overwhelming experience. Chhaya could not figure it out if it was a daydream or if it had really happened. Exactly that Kim was before her— the Kim she craved for, the very Kim as she had thought him to be. How nice, he offered to take her on a ride!

: "Where shall I go now at such an odd hour? I'll tell you whenever I need. My jewel, my wealth; you must not drive speedily." She said affectionately with delight.

: "Look here." Kim drew back her mother's attention to the mobile phone. Handing it over to her, he offered liberally, "Would you like to talk with anyone?"

Chhaya saw the small gadget. She had thought of going for such a thing. She again felt that there wasn't so vast a world around her for which such an instrument was essential. Still she wished to have one.

: "See, how to dial." He showed how to use that and bringing to his ear he said, "Uncle, I am Kim here. I reached just now. No, not at all; there wasn't any problem on the way. Yes, she is here with me. She would like to talk to you."

Handing over the mobile phone to her he said, "Speak, the younger uncle is at the other end. Say 'Hello".

Chhaya would feel shy to go to school by motorcycle the next day. She said, "You go to the college by your bike. The school is at a stone's throw; I will walk up the distance."

Kim paid a deaf ear to what she said. Waiting outside

on the bike he called her once or twice, "Come quickly; why do you make a delay?"

She got on to the bike intending not to hurt Kim's sentiments. Kim cautioned her, "Beware of your saree; it might get caught in the wheel if you are careless."

Kim enjoyed a special prestige in the college for these two instruments. No other student possessed such things. Possibly for that reason, he contested for the post of the General Secretary of the College Union. But when the canvassing was at its peak, he withdrew his candidature.

: "Hey, what has happened to you?" Chhaya asked feeling worried.

Kim appeared grave. He looked as if he would start weeping soon. He kept gazing at his mother unmindfully for some moments. He was perhaps searching for the cause of his misfortune that stood as a big stumbling block on the path of his progress.

: "I won't go to this college anymore." Kim announced.

The voice that came from an ice packed tunnel could scarcely reach its opening. It got lost amid the dark silence and utter disappointment. Chhaya did not ask why he resolved like that.

That evening Sony reached. She might get some information from Sony who continued as a plus-two second-year student there in that college. Sony looked at her aunt for a moment and then buried her face. She was not that sprightly, fresh and chatty like she was on other days.

It would have been better if Chhaya had not asked anything after seeing her in that condition. She hoped that Sony's report would be something different from the reason she had guessed.

: "Aunty!" Sony addressed her. For a moment she

kept mum burying her face once again. So dense was the silence that there could be no room for any conversation. Chhaya marked with concern that Sony wiped her tear with a finger. The silence of the room was overflooded with tears.

: "Aunty, please don't ask me anything; I can't say that."

Sony's effort showed that speech making required a great effort. She raised her head and looked at her aunt with endless empathy.

After Sony had left, Chhaya felt how the entire energy and enthusiasm could go waste without her knowledge and could transform her into a motionless mould. Till nine at night there had been no trace of Kim. During the election campaign, his contestant would have told something insulting. It was not difficult to guess that. Kim could not have faced that horrible thing.

Chhaya was the only weakness of Kim's life. She was the shame and insult for him. She had never felt weak or disgraced after the rape. Astounding the family members and all other acquaintances, she kept her head high everywhere. She was not the culprit; it was someone else. The power and inspiration to struggle and protest originated from the source of that thought; from a strong sense of revolt for having been a prey.

No, it would not be possible to take it that way. The anguish and injustice that Chhaya had been a victim of could never be transmitted to Kim in any different manner because Kim himself had been victimized for being Chhaya's son. Possibly, he thought like this. There was nothing unpleasant in Chhaya's getting married but why she became a mother. Kim would never be able to free himself from the tag that his mother had once been a rape victim.

Perhaps, Kim had become an object of ridicule under the ink of an unwanted and shameful stamp.

: "This boy is weak and has become unjustifiably sensitive." Chhaya said to herself. The revolt within him should have been against the society. Then only he could have been able to confront the insulting and humiliating elements. That way he could offend that power and create within it the sense of guilt. Kim was not able to do that nor could he do it ever. He would flutter, being crucified by such shame and insult and would never be able to assert himself. He would remain a shrunken self, a cursed spite whom everything would appear vast and full of ridicules.

It was not possible to be optimistic about Kim anymore.

Was there any clue to a solution? She felt lost! Chhaya calculated how far it would be effective. She was prepared to get herself lost a thousand times for Kim's sake. But where was the possibility of the extinction of her history with her death? Maybe, she would not be there to care about the direction, the momentum and the colour of Kim's way of life. She would have got lost by then. Kim's sighs impregnated with anguish and insult could never touch her then. But that would never be the solution to Kim's problem.

In fact, he did not go to college. He looked dejected, as it were, he was a fragment. Although young, Kim had a history but no future. He moved about without any hustle or bustle. He had the entire time with him. He had no design to give shape to the plan of any activity. He looked unrelated and depressed having the least interest in being connected with something or somebody. His loneliness and alienation was a hulking wound within him. He would rear that wound to keep it fresh and suppurating out of which he would get a strange pleasure. He was a victim for which he was not at all responsible. He would create that impression.

But before whom and why did he create such an impression? There would be none but Chhaya to see that. How did Kim derive any pleasure creating the impression before his mother that he was a victim?

But another aspect became clear to Chhaya. At times Kim became restless and impatient which pierced deep into his lonely alienation. He would possibly feel his bones and muscles to have a maddening spirit which found no way of escape. That was nothing less than confinement. He had been in a state of indecisiveness in adopting any definite approach even after having freedom from that confinement.

That boy was not only weak but also preferred to remain confined, although he was burning within. He had some dangerous element within him. It was not possible to guess what would happen when.

: "Will you not go to college, really?" Chhaya asked expressing concern and anxiety.

He was cleaning the motorcycle carefully near the well. He would wash it with detergent mixed water in every week or once in three-four days if soiled. It shined always creating the illusion that it had been fresh from the showroom. Of late, all his interest and activity centred on keeping the bike clean from which he got satisfaction.

With the wet cloth in hand, he looked at Chhaya. He said again before resuming his work, "College? I do not have to go to college anymore." After a slight pause, he said to himself, "College! What would I do there?"

: "Alright; if not in this college, you can get yourself admitted in some other college." Chhaya said that as a consolation.

: "What would I do in a college?" Almost he challenged her.

Chhaya did not know the answer to that question. She said, "You could do something at least. How long will you have this desultory life and move about? Losing all interests, you will be tired and bored of everything."

The bike was clean and shining to his satisfaction. He had to say something; and for that, he said, "Sure, I will do something which I am yet to decide. But I will do something."

Sony passed the plus-two examination in her second attempt. She declared that she would not carry on her studies any further. She took over the house management from Appa who suffered from arthritic pain at the lumber and genicular regions.

Kim would eat, sleep and while away the time at home. He would go out with his bike in the afternoon and would return after half an hour or at nine or ten at night as he pleased. Where were you for so long? The answer to this question had been like- "Just like that I had gone; what would you get out of that?"

Chhaya lost her patience when it became past ten in the night. She had finished cooking by nine. The correction work had also been over much before. TV programme was not adequate enough to hold her attention any more. She would sit and try to read something but frequent yawns would interrupt that. She would become conscious at times that she was dosing.

The exterior walls of the house had not been plastered. The door and window panels had not been painted too. She felt vexed for having absorbed herself in useless worries. The village had been overpowered by deep sleep at that hour of the night. Kim was not seen. His bike sound could be audible from a distance due to silence, but that night the silence lay as if without any bound for eternity obstructing the infiltration of any sound.

Her impatience soon changed into concerns and premonitions. The drowsiness vanished, and the rate of her heart beat went up. She felt thirsty. Her throat parched. Nothing in the semblance of silence remained there. A dry crashing and clanging sound occupied the space from there up to the sky and the horizon. Very soon it was converted into a dreadfully horrific sound. For the first time, Chhaya felt the newly constructed concrete walls, floors and roof of her house melting down. She, being alone and helpless, hung in the vast void of the space. The absolutely new experience had a speciality about it which created a vague premonition that something terrible had already happened somewhere, and Kim was at its centre— ruined and shattered. There was no message from Kim's mobile.

Bike accident! Nothing to think except that was possible for Chhaya. Where and in what condition was Kim? Did he commit any violence with anyone? Everything was possible.

She got younger brother Pravir at the other end after dialing for three or four times. Her fear and anxiety was at its climax. Kim had not gone there. Pravir also expressed apprehension.

His drowsy voice was no more heard. Trying to console her he said, "Listen, you won't gain anything by crying like this. The problem is that it's one o'clock at night. It is not possible to do anything at this time. Still, let me see if anything can be done."

Chhaya got no information from the known numbers of his friends. No one had met Kim that day.

Did such a big boy go missing? The dark and silent

night seemed enigmatic and merciless with all indifference. Nowhere amid its vastness was there a slight trace of empathy or solace. As if that vast silence kept its mouth so endlessly wide open that anyone would get lost there.

Chhaya's fear and anxiety had already infected Abhay's family. Abhay had come there. He was left with no words to console her. As per his advice, Sony stayed with her. All the families of the village had already come to know about that by daybreak. Kim had been missing since the previous night.

It was as if all her veins and arteries would burst and shatter owing to utter anxiety and restlessness, and all the blood would drain out. All her sinews would break into pieces. No more would Chhaya be able to hold so much of anxiety and apprehensions within her. She ran within the room and rambled about on the road with rapt ears to hear the sound of the bike. Had the motorcycle forgotten the way or had it no willingness to come under its own roof? Or; was it that Kim had forgotten the path or was not willing to come to his known lap? Chhaya was about to faint.

Pravir's message to give her protection was, "Is there anyone with you?" His voice reflected urgency and excitement.

: "No." Chhaya wanted to hear intently. Perchance there would be any difficulty in hearing, she kept her blood circulation and breathing suspended at that climactic moment. Like giving some hope, she said, "I am on the road, all alone."

: "Listen," the instruction was from Pravir's side. He said, "Kim is in trouble. The Police is searching for him. I will keep him in a safe place."

The phone was disconnected. Numerous questions blurted out silently from her mouth and met a head-on crash with the mute mobile phone. First, she felt a little relieved. But by and by, her anxiety became more acute on hearing about the police search. She in that condition got ready to go to the Bus stand. She needed detailed information about Kim. She was not aware of what instruction she gave to Sony; or if at all she had given any.

She was face to face with the police officer while coming out of the house. There were two constables with the officer.

How one looks like when one becomes bloodless and lifeless—one could have a better idea if he took a look at Chhaya at that time. She would confront death as it is a must; she could stand before a criminal, a rapist and before a ferocious beast as there would be no way out to escape. But could she stand before the police-the police out to find out Kim? The world got lost. Where in which unknown realm the wind got lost? The light faded away to the west. Before her were three hard-hearted police men in khaki uniform.

: "Are you Kim's mother, Chhaya madam?" He enquired.

: "Yes," she wanted to say, but she could not know for certain if she could do it.

: "Is he at home now?"

: "No." She said in an almost sobbing voice. Chhaya was again amid the crashing and clanging sounds.

: "Exactly at what time did he leave the house yesterday?" The officer gave the indication that his face would not have a smile or any sign of sympathy at such a moment like that.

: "About five or six in the evening." The blood stream that had missed the path within her was becoming active.

: "And has not returned after that, has he?" There was no change in his style of questioning.

: "Has not returned." Chhaya was getting back the respiration that she had kept suspended. Her nerves started to come round. The mother in her was becoming active to create a safety ring around her son in danger.

: "We will raid the house." He announced and instructed the constables- "Search him out."

: "What is the allegation against Kim? " Chhaya asked the officer about to enter the house.

: "Don't you know it? Really?" He asked.

: "No." Chhaya emphasized in a tone of appeal.

: "There is rape allegation against Kim." The officer said. He gave another piece of information, "A college girl has filed the FIR."

It was not only a terrible tornado; it was a devastative earthquake too. Chhaya was split into pieces. The shattered fragments were quite incapable to help her stand. Firstly, she leaned against the wall. After a few moments, she collapsed on the floor.

A thousand flaws were created on the horizon. The sky seemed like a thatched roof. The earth cracked. Through all these gaps— from the top, from below and from all the corners sallied countless criminals. All the Chhayas and all the girls of the world were being ravished by their bestiality. Their mouths were gagged and hands tied. There were wounds all over the body. The bleeding was unwilling to stop.

Chhaya's body horripilated even in that helpless and unconscious state. A bellow from within her was about to give an SOS call.

Rape! The very word is impregnated with horrendous scenes. Rape! There is a lethal experience in this single small word. Chhaya was surrounded by that very scene and that very experience again after so many years. It lasted till then for so many years. Fear and protest came back to her again. She was a victim to that bestiality once again!

: "Aunty! " Chhaya came back to the living present. She gave a stupid look at Sony and drank the glass of water she had held. Absorbed, she looked at Sony's face. Sony could not understand why aunty held her face in her cupped palms. She burst into tears and asked with unforeseen sympathy, "Are you alright, aunty? Has anything happened to you?"

Chhaya did not try to get up even. The fragmented vanished world was collecting itself again to its previous whole. Appa and Abhay bhai stood by her. A few ladies were also there and there on the road.

Chhaya said to Sony, "My mobile was somewhere here. Find it out for me."

On getting that she said, "Bhai and Appa, I need to consult you. Sony, you go now."

She went way. Chhaya stood up firmly. The ground under her feet was stable and steady as there was no earthquake any more. All her limbs were active. Despite the hunger and sleeplessness, she looked bright, as if her face was brightened up by a halo of lustre.

: "Who would you telephone to?" Appa said in a suppressed voice like transferring some secret.

: "I guess where the criminal would be at this time." She seemed sure.

: "What, do you want to help them catch your son?" There was fear and disbelief in Abhay bhai's tone.

: "He is a criminal." Chhaya affirmed adding, "He has been alleged of rape. It is necessary that the police should arrest him."

: "Have you lost all your senses?" Abhay shouted.

"Can you do like this being the mother? If Kim has done something like this, some arrangement can be made."

: "Arrangement! For that only, the criminals are never caught. Only for this sort of arrangement or system the police go on searching indefinitely when the rapists are there under their nose. That is the system. It is there. For that, the rape victim will go to the Police Station bearing the wounds all over her body to lodge the FIR. And would again go there to inquire as to why the culprits could not be arrested; she would file the petition at the SP's. "Search is going on; the criminals are not identified. They haven't left any clue through which it would be easy to get at them." And then she has to appeal at the court of the Magistrate.

Perhaps it is the system that determines the victim's way. Chhaya felt the pain for the victim. The criminal is not missing. He is there and has been identified. It only remains to nab him.

Chhaya looked at Abhay bhai. Appa's lumber and genicular pain was unbearably severe. Chhaya gave her word to them that she would not do any such thing which would put Kim in trouble. Her other promise was that she would go to their house to have her meal after her daily chores.

Chhaya was in the infinite space after they had left her. She was dwindling and at the same time mustering courage to take a decisive step. Her blood cells, arteries, and veins had never been so brisk and alert hitherto.

Not only the members of Abhay bhai's family; many people of the village also could not believe their eyes. About one o'clock in the afternoon, the police van stopped in front of Chhaya's house. Shutting the doors and windows madam kept herself waiting outside her house for the police van. Getting into the van she directed them to move on.

No one had ever seen such an expedition to find out the culprit.

After half an hour or so, Chhaya was before Pravir. "Tell me, where you have concealed the criminal; otherwise, all the family members including you will be arrested on the charge of giving shelter to a culprit."

Pravir could not recognize his appa of that moment and could not make out exactly what she said. He looked confounded. Subsequently, he trembled out of anger and hatred. He asked, "Are you a mother or a monster?"

There was no necessity of much exertion or warning. By three o'clock the handcuffed culprit was already there in the police van. Relieved and slightly obliged, the police officer said, "We thank you, madam, for your cooperation. But we will be straight to the Police Station, and from there I will arrange to send you back."

Kim seemed calm and unprotesting although he looked bloodless. He had no plan to escape. He saw his mother and buried his face. There was no reaction with him; no sign of repentance either for committing the crime. He was not also elated for what he had committed.

Chhaya kept herself seated on the bench on the veranda of the Police Station. No more would be the brisk and alert blood cells and arteries be active. Their role had come to an end forever. Chhaya was only a lifeless, hollow frame. There had been no sense faculty left in benumbed Chhaya after the breath-arresting and maddening incident. She had no verve to figure out what had happened and what it implied.

Time was slipping off. She had no eagerness to return. She was in such a state that she could not say why and where she was.

She had a vague feeling of someone touching her feet

to salute her. Before her was the hazy figure of the man paying regards to her.

: "I am one of your old students." The voice was indistinct as if that came from some other planet, "I have my bike; I'll leave you at home. Grant me this privilege please."

While on the bike, she was aware of some facts. She was Chhaya madam, a teacher by profession at Chandanpur who had lost her husband many years ago. And now she was returning home after losing Kim, her only son.

On reaching home, she offered a glass of water to her student whose name she couldn't remember and advised him to drive carefully on his way back. She could recognize the Head Master but she was too exhausted to say something to him; unlocking the door, she straight entered her house. She went to Abhay bhai's house at about eight thirty for dinner.

Switching off all the lights of all rooms, Chhaya sat on the bed in her room. The wall clock sounded like the heart beats of the sleeping universe. She listened to this particular sound like listening to it for the first time. The copies of the students were there on the table close to her bed. She had already corrected them. She was surprised to know that it was in her memory. She looked at the motionless TV screen.

She got up to drink some water. Till then it had not struck eleven even. Switching off the light, she lay down on the bed. The ticking of the wall clock was not heard anymore. Then there was a strange sound. The sounds of the motor vehicles, the cry of newborn Kim, the giggling of her ME school friends, the coughing of father Gananath, the masons' conversations at the time of the construction of that house and the breaking sound of teacups- all got jumbled up to build up that strange sound. She heard it.

Besides these sounds she could see a variety of scenes- bad road, the prayer of the students, the idol of Saraswati and Kim's motor bike.

Again she got up from the bed and drank some water. There was no restlessness in her; she had no inclination to cry. Everything was normal and undisturbed. Everything was calm and fixed after a lot of stirs and anxieties. Notwithstanding the peacefulness, she could not fall asleep. Its reason was not known.

She tried to sleep. How long should she have slept? She got up late in the next morning when the domestic help knocked at the wooden grill gate repeatedly. She was face to face with the lighted world.

She prepared a cup of tea. While enjoying the tea she marked that the plants looked fresh although the soil in the vase was dried up. They bore flowers also.

But she was slightly taken aback while combing her hair before the mirror. Some locks had already turned grey without her knowledge. The eyes having black patches around had also shrunken on her wrinkled face. Such a big change only within a day!

She would go to the Police Station to visit Kim. Then she would prepare for the future actions. Kim! Chhaya was neither emotive nor repenting. The identity of her son called Kim had been lost within the identity of the previous day's culprit. But now, Kim was only Kim, nothing except her son.

While cogitating on the future plans, how she was to prepare herself and what steps to take she came out to the veranda. Someone wanted to see her.

: "Madam, my name is Vicky; I work in a TV channel.

I had come yesterday but didn't wish to disturb you, as you were terribly tired on your return from the Police Station."

He stopped and looked at Chhaya's face. There was no sign of disgust or interest. She waited to know precisely what business Vicky had with her.

: "An extraordinary event!" Vicky said with love and regards adding further, "It has some social and humanistic issues in this. Madam, I have come to take your interview. Would you please share half an hour's time with me?"

Chhaya looked at Vicky's face for some moments and expressed her indifference, "I had also heard about the social and human aspects in the past. I haven't given any thought on that. I did whatever I deemed fit and appropriate. But, don't mind, for it is not possible to cooperate with you. There are certain important things at hand to do. Even when I had no work to do, I had never been interested in the past for an interview. And I am not interested for it today either."

Vicky didn't feel hurt or offended. Had there been the privilege, he would have kept on looking at Chhaya, year after year for many years indefatigably as he knew it for sure that the camera was too incapable an instrument to capture the things he saw and experienced.

GLOSSARY

Appa-	Elder sister/ sister-in-law
Barapalli Latrine-	Indian style toilet sheet first made at Barapalli, Sambalpur around mid-1800 AD
Bindi-	A small coloured mark that is worn between the eyebrows ,especially by Hindu women to show that they are married. Chunri- A long scarf worn by women over kameez
Dedhashura-	Husband's elder brother. In Odisha they do not see or touch the younger brother's wife (Bhai bohu)
Gherao-	To prevent someone to come out
Havildar-	A Head constable
Kameez-	A cassock like knee-long long dress worn by women
Lungi-	A garment similar to a sarong worn around the waist; it extends up to the ankle.
Mehndi-	A herbal solution used by women to paint pictures on palms
Mridang-	A barrel-shaped double-headed drum with one head larger than the other, an Indian musical instrument
Namaskar-	Salutation
Papad-	A thin, flat, round, crispy food stuff usually deep fried or roasted

Pooja/Puja-	worship
Prasad-	The Sacrament which is not just a food to eat but the physical presence of God's blessing.
Rakhi-	A piece of coloured thread the Indian sisters tie on the wrist of brothers on the July Full Moon day
Serbet-	Homemade cold drink
Sudasha Brata-	Worshipping Goddess Laxmi on Thursday that falls on the 10th day of the crescent moon
Taraat-	White flowers
Tulsi-	A holy plant worshipped by Hindus
Vouja-	Wife of elder brother

BLACK EAGLE BOOKS

www.blackeaglebooks.org
info@blackeaglebooks.org

Black Eagle Books, an independent publisher, was founded as
a nonprofit organization in April, 2019. It is our mission to
connect and engage the Indian diaspora and the world at large
with the best of works of world literature published on a
collaborative platform, with special emphasis on
foregrounding Contemporary Classics and New Writing.